Praise for the Award-Winning
A Doctor a Day

"Just the thought of getting hit by a malpractice suit is like being stripped bare and hit so hard in the gut that you are wrenched over and staggering. It rips at every story you tell yourself about how you are good enough to be trusted with another's life. And it feels so blindly unfair. This story accurately portrays the mental and physical toil that dealing death and dying continuously coupled with the ever present scimitar of a malpractice suit hanging overhead can take on the physician."

— *Radiation Oncologist (name withheld)*

"Dr. Mansheim's compelling novel describes accurately the pressures of primary care medical practice. His protagonist, Dr. Luke James, suffers the consequences of unending psychological stress. Though a fictional story, the experiences leading to burnout and depression ring true. A must read— especially for anyone having a hard time finding a primary care physician. I'm looking forward to his sequels, which I hope will delve further into the administrative, economic, and organizational stressors of the job."

— *Gib Morrow, M.D.*

Praise for the Award-Winning
A Doctor a Day

"Many of the realities of modern medical practice: the rigors of medical training, medical-social injustice, end-of-life issues, the vagaries of medical insurance, experimental medicine, physician burnout and the stress of medical malpractice litigation, among others are captured by Dr. Mansheim in this short, insightful novel. A rewarding and important read for anyone interested in these timely topics."

— Stephen H. Zinner, M.D.
Charles S. Davidson
Distinguished Professor of Medicine,
Harvard Medical School

"…an honest and insightful portrayal of a medical practitioner's daily struggles with the inevitability of death…poignant, exceptionally daunting, and valiant…"

— Chanticleer Reviews

"Every patient should read **A Doctor a Day**."

— Jeffrey L. Harrison, Stephen O'Connell Chair
Professor of Law, University of Florida College of Law

A Timely Topic

"…the medical profession consistently hovers near the top of occupations with the highest risk of death by suicide…perhaps a doctor a day. A reasonable assumption is that underreporting of suicide as the cause of death by sympathetic colleagues certifying death may well skew these statistics; consequently, the real incidence of physician suicide is probably somewhat higher than the prevailing estimate."

— Louise B. Andrew, M.D., J.D.
Medscape, June 12, 2017

"More than one million Americans lose their physicians to suicide every year so we must take this seriously. If not for the individual, the public health implications of losing that many physicians when we already have a physician shortage…And that's not even counting the medical students that die by suicide."

— Pamela Wible, M.D.
*We Lose a Medical School Full of Physicians
Every Year to Suicide:
An Interview with Dr. Pamela Wible*
by Christine Sinsky, M.D.
from the
American Medical Association
TEDMED talk, Nov. 21, 2015

A Doctor a Day

A Novel

by
Bernard Mansheim, M.D.

Prior to enrolling in medical school, Bernard Mansheim received a Bachelor's degree in English Literature. After he completed medical school and post-graduate training, he began his career with academic appointments at Harvard Medical School and the University of Florida College of Medicine as an Infectious Disease specialist. He left academic medicine for private practice, and then became Chief Medical Officer of a national health insurance company for the last ten years of his career.

He has lectured extensively on various topics, including medical ethics and managed health care, and has served as an expert witness in medical malpractice cases. He received awards from the Florida Medical Association and the Florida Hospital Association for a monthly newspaper column he wrote for a few years.

After his thirty-five year career, he became a health care consultant, has been a member of several non-profit boards, and continues to volunteer weekly as a physician at a free medical clinic.

His outside interests have included marathon running, golf and other sports, travel, and writing novels. He lives with his wife in Charleston, South Carolina and Santa Fe, New Mexico.

JAMES ISLAND PRESS
An imprint of Sillan Pace Brown Group LLC
1626 NW Thurman Street
Portland, Oregon 97209

www.SillanPaceBrown.com

First Edition, **ISBN**-13: 978-1-64058-000-8
ISBN-10: 1-64058-000-X

1. Medical fiction. 2. Physicians' lives –Fiction.
3. Doctors dealing with death, & dying—Fiction.
4. Literary. 5. Suicide—Fiction. 6. Physician &
patient—Fiction. 7. Medical law—Fiction.
8. Modern Medical Practices—Fiction

Published in the United States of America by
James Island Press, a member of Sillan Pace Brown
Group (USA), LLC, 2017

For Denise, my soul mate

A Doctor a Day

A Novel

Book One in the
Everydoctor Series

Bernard Mansheim, M.D.

A note from the publisher:

Please note that quotation marks to distinguish dialogue are purposely missing from this work of fiction at the author's request.

Whether across death's threshold we step from
life to life, or whether we go whence we shall not
return, even to the land of darkness,
as darkness itself, he cannot tell.

— *Sir William Osler*

Chapter 1

July 1987 (Medical Practice—Year Ten)

Luke had been sitting a long time on the dark screened porch, staring north across the yard toward Wainwright's Prairie. He saw only blackness. The marsh noises were surprisingly loud— creatures owned the night. He listened to the waves of sounds as they waxed and waned in an atonal orchestration, punctuated with random pauses. Some ghostly conductor out there directed the symphony.

The chorus of spring peepers, tiny frogs that were rarely seen, sounded like a box full of newborn chicks, their individual cheeps coalescing into a high-pitched din. The cicadas with their vibrating timbals kept up a constant buzz, like the drone string of a sitar. Kamikaze insects took turns pelting the screen. There were other, larger nocturnal creatures out there: raccoons, possums, and armadillos, all scrabbling through fallen tree branches without a care in the world.

The enervating northern Florida heat glued Luke to the chair. He sat in a torpor, bathed in sweat. He tried to make his mind blank and focus on the earthy smells and incessant sounds of the summer night. He pleaded with himself to shut out his conscious thoughts and let his brain rest.

Moonlight backlit a massive live oak tree that stood in the yard. He focused on the thick clumps of Spanish moss that draped the giant, ancient branches. The old tree's few low, sweeping limbs cantilevered out from the trunk nearly a hundred feet. Those powerful arms had an unimaginable inner strength that had withstood the inexorable pull of gravity, unfazed by lightning, disease, or hurricanes. The moss was a fur blanket that clung but remained independent, an epiphyte hitching a ride yet minding its own business.

He had often marveled at the permanence and strength of that tree. In a way he saw it as an older brother, somehow meant to protect him. But the solace he had felt and the energy he had drawn from his arboreal companion had begun to slip away.

He shifted his weight in the chair and crossed his legs, trying to call forth the spirit of the Wakulla band of Seminoles, who once had encamped nearby, long since brutally killed and starved out. He yearned for some mystical shaman to appear and utter a few healing magical words or wave a protective talisman. He felt trapped, as though Lucite walls were closing in from all sides, getting nearer with each heartbeat, despite his view of the moon-bathed grassland that spread out in front of him.

The door to the living room opened. He heard the worried voice of his wife.

Luke, come to bed. You need to be rested for the trial.

In bed, he lay with eyes wide open, staring at the black void. Betsy's breathing was deep and rhythmic. No other sounds disturbed the darkness. Inside his head was a world alive with a cacophony of voices, like a crowd of people coming and going, all talking at once. He saw blackness outside, while flames of light exploded in his brain.

Usually, sleep came easily to Luke. He would wait for the characters inside his head, manically active in ways never experienced in his conscious world, to wind down. He'd always been fascinated by this panorama, as though he were a spectator of his own large, unorganized debate party. Then sleep would come, descending like a curtain slowly dropping to the stage as the lights faded.

But not this night. The usual craziness was crowded out by thoughts of the day. His mind raced obsessively as he replayed all the parts of an earlier conversation. He turned over and saw the demonic, red clock digits mocking him—3:18 a.m.

He quietly rolled out of bed and dragged himself downstairs to the living room where he sank heavily into an old wicker easy chair. The field-stone fireplace rose twelve feet to the open-beam ceiling. It stood before him like a large hand on his head that offered a peculiar sense of security. His arms tingled; a draft blew gently on them. His eyes felt sandy and his body was bone tired, yet he remained hypervigilant. He listened to the arthritic creaks of the old log home. From the black void, he revisited the events of the day, because he could not escape them.

The courtroom was antiquated and paneled in dark wood. The ceilings were at least twenty feet high, an homage to the days before air-conditioning. Ceiling fans turned lazily, moving the stagnant air hardly at all. The black-robed judge perched six feet above the lawyers, the jury, the defendant, and the smattering of spectators. From his lofty bench, he solemnly peered over his half-glasses, looking down his nose at the proceedings. He might be taken for a medieval, robed bishop, sternly observing his flock, all neatly arranged in wooden pews behind an altar rail. The symbolism seemed a bit trite, even remotely humorous.

Instead, Luke, from his position as defendant, reckoned it more as basketball court. In fact, he thought it would be better served with a hoop at each end and bleachers along the sides. The pews could be donated to a church. As it was, the whole scene had uncomfortable religious overtones that spooked him. He pictured the court reporter, jury, lawyers, and other cast members as silent monks bowing before their abbot. In this secular tribunal, he awaited legal and moral judgment from on high, figuratively, or maybe literally.

He snapped out of his cynical digression. His super-ego chastised his wisecracking id, as he admonished himself to stay focused.

The witness box to the left of the judge was equipped with a microphone. The jury, seated just beyond, sideways, could see everything: the judge, the plaintiff and defendant, the lawyers, and the spectators. Two rows, twelve jurors in all, got a close-up view of all the actors in this surreal drama. The windows were uncovered and elevated, like a prison cell, allowing light but no view.

The judge opened the proceedings by looking at the jury.

Good morning, ladies and gentlemen. You have been selected as jury in the matter of Cartwright v. Dr. Luke James. Dr. James is charged with malpractice. He has entered a plea of "not guilty" to the charge.

The plaintiff's attorney presented the case in painstaking detail, calling one witness after another. Frequent objections by the defense to fine points in the testimony interrupted the flow throughout the morning.

Luke spent the time obsessing about the opening statement and was jolted from his reverie when the judge called for a lunch break. The case continued as the late-afternoon summer sun created streaks of light. He could see dust motes floating on the broad beams. It was that lazy time of day in the Deep South when time stood still. The transition between day and evening, when Cuban Americans in Miami downed a *cafecito*, a thimble-size booster dose of caffeine.

Coffee was not available in the courtroom. The jury looked glassy-eyed as if they, too, were wishing the day was over. The plaintiff's attorney strutted back and forth laying out his case. Luke, bolt upright in the hard oak chair, glared at him—an inexpert hex. The attorney referred to him as *the defendant*.

Two days ago he'd been a doctor. He'd dedicated his career to helping people, to saving lives, to relieving suffering. Now he was a *defendant.*

He made subtle, sidelong glances at the jury. *Should I stare at them? Smile? Leer? Nod? No, I'd better not make eye contact. Or should I?* He wanted to tell them that he was still a doctor, not an alleged criminal. Those twelve ordinary-looking people, some now almost half-asleep, could have been his patients. If one had a heart attack right there in the courtroom, he would jump from his chair and start resuscitation. He would shout orders: lay him down, loosen his tie, call 9-1-1. He almost wished for it. Then they would see him as a doctor again.

No one on the jury fainted or cried out with chest pain.

Luke remained a defendant. He was relegated to thoughts of how to convince these twelve people that he was not guilty. He knew that presumption of innocence was fundamental to the American legal system. But denying his guilt seemed to acknowledge that guilt was a possibility. Maybe it would appear to them as a false denial. How, then, could he declare his innocence? His mind argued in circles.

For the thousandth time, he pulled himself into a straight-backed position. He had purposely attired himself in a plain charcoal suit, a starched white shirt, and a nondescript blue tie. His hands were clasped uncomfortably, almost prayer-like, on the table. They suddenly felt like an awkward accessory. He could not find another place for them.

He talked to himself.

Try to look confident but not supercilious. Maybe they sense my fear. I want them to be like my patients, who look at me, trust my words, maybe feel a little unbalanced by my white coat and their need to believe that I could answer their questions, reassure them, diagnose their problems, treat them, cure them.

He needed the jurors to believe he was their doctor, not a defendant.

Yet his mind tossed on a sea of doubt. He began to worry that his very presence might mean to the jurors that he was more likely than not to be guilty. He stole glances. *Look at them*, he thought. *They look like my patients—fat, thin, black, white, some probably happy to make the few dollars they get for sitting in judgment all day long, others impatient at the waste of their precious time.*

He perceived a kind expression here, a stern one there. No real smiles. Can they know what I am thinking? What are they thinking? Do they resent doctors because of a bad experience in the past? Maybe they admire doctors.

He continued to obsess until he heard a firm voice: The plaintiff calls Dr. Alan Fleming.

A slight man in a navy blue suit and polished black shoes strode through the wooden gate and mounted the steps to the witness stand, the expert testifying for the plaintiff. He was bald but with a ring of hair that gave a tonsure effect. He had a finicky, perfectly trimmed moustache and rimless glasses.

His upturned lip was a subtle sneer, as if over-compensating for his diminutive stature. He raised his right hand, placed his left hand on the Bible, and looked down his sharply pointed nose while he vowed to tell the truth.

Luke—the doctor, now the defendant—was at once angry and deflated. This pompous academic would likely collect a hefty fee to testify. And on what did he base his testimony? No doubt he had reviewed countless pages of medical records, read depositions extracted from unsuspecting aides at the nursing home who were easily tripped up by a clever lawyer, and gotten testimonials from a family who saw a pot of gold.

And of course the plaintiff's attorney had coached the expert witness, whose feigned omniscience was buttressed by a mountain of academic publications and a faculty title. *Had he ever had his hands on my patient . . . or any patient since his medical training, for that matter? Did he recoil at the stench of stale urine in the nursing home? Did he take the late-night calls about confused screaming and crying? No, chances are he'd never gotten his hands dirty.*

Powerless, Luke knew that the jury would decide his fate based on the testimony of this man, fully ten years his junior, and had never seen his patient and knew nothing of the months of care and concern that were embedded forever in his own memory. He recalled reading that a jury's decision often came down to opening and closing statements, and to expert witness testimony. The rest was filler.

Who could he tell that this testimony could tear apart a reputation built on years of study, training, late nights, dying patients, and too much time away from his family members, missing their father and husband? Who would understand the magnetic, relentless hold of medical practice? No, he could only sit in silence, watching the "expert" know-it-all weasel revel in his elevated perch.

Dr. Fleming, tell the court about the deceased.

The expert adjusted himself, took a sip from a water glass and cozied up to the microphone.

Lucille Cartwright, as I understand it, was an eighty-five-year-old woman and had resided at the Hill Manor Nursing Home for about two years. She suffered from advanced Alzheimer 's disease, a form of severe dementia.

She was bedridden and unable to care for herself, totally dependent on the nursing staff. She was incapable of feeding herself and too feeble to complain of pain or discomfort. She was disoriented, and incontinent of urine and stool. She received nourishment through a nasogastric tube because she could not swallow.

The attorney interrupted. Nasogastric tube?

Yes, it is a feeding tube threaded through the nose into the stomach. Liquid nutrients and medications are advanced through the tube several times a day. He continued. The nurses turned her regularly, to shift her position in bed and to change her diapers.

What else, Dr. Fleming?

Her urine was drained from her bladder through a tube. And, unfortunately, from lying in the same position for over a year or two, she had developed a large wound on her buttocks, almost twenty centimeters in diameter. It was infected and malodorous.

Malodorous?

It means foul-smelling. It stank of rotting flesh, and was so deep it extended down to her sacral bone.

Luke sat in his chair, listening, as the expert continued to paint a gruesome picture. It was slow torture. Disgust welled up inside him for the self-styled expert continuing to construct a distorted story meant only to place blame. He sat pinned to his chair in the crosshairs. The expert could explain to the jury the meaning of four-syllable medical words like malodorous. But he conveyed no awareness that the patient's terrible condition had existed long before Luke ever agreed to assume her care.

Dr. Fleming continued.

The wound was packed with gauze several times a day. She also had two deep wounds on her hips, called decubitus ulcers or pressure sores. She had developed a high fever and had lapsed into a coma. Her blood pressure was falling. Her doctor was called, and he told the nurses to keep her comfortable.

Her doctor is the defendant seated over there? The attorney pointed toward Luke.

Yes, that's him.

The defendant you have identified, Dr. James, did not advise the nursing staff to send her by ambulance to the hospital? The attorney's voice pretended at disbelief.

No, he explicitly instructed them not to send her to the emergency room. Not to give her anti-biotics to treat her life-threatening infection.

Fleming's voice took on a strident, staged quality.

Just keep her comfortable, he said. He told them she was near death. They did what was ordered, and six hours later she was dead.

There was a calculated pause.

In your expert opinion, Dr. Fleming, does the care rendered by the defendant, her doctor, constitute malpractice?

The witness leaned forward, closer to the microphone.

Yes.

Thank you, Dr. Fleming. The plaintiff rests.

The sun faded as if on cue. The expert witness walked out. The room was silent.

The judge spoke. Court will be adjourned until tomorrow at nine a.m.

He tapped the gavel, rose, and strode out the back door. The jury filed out through a side door. The lawyers gathered their papers.

Luke sat, stunned, hurt, numb. He waved his lawyer away. He wanted to tell someone he was a doctor, not a defendant. He mouthed the words: *a doctor, not a defendant*.

Chapter 2

July 1972 (Internship)

The dreams and aspirations Luke had all the way back to childhood had finally come to fruition. Medicine had been the only profession he ever considered. His father—a doctor and a kind man, long deceased from cancer—would have been proud. This was Luke's chance to carry the legacy forward.

The first few rows of the hospital auditorium filled slowly. It was the final stop on the morning-long orientation for the new interns. Along with nineteen other medical interns, Luke had undergone a health screening and a trip to the hospital laundry to pick up a package wrapped in green that included standard-issue uniforms. Separated out from the surgical and pediatric interns, the medical interns gathered in the auditorium.

Luke picked a seat on the aisle where he could look over the group. Everyone wore a thin disguise of nonchalance as they lounged in the seats, sharing inane comments that reflected their poorly hidden anxiety. He heard occasional muffled sounds over the paging system and the distant wailing of an ambulance. His mind wandered.

Here we are at medical boot camp. We lined up for our whites: three smocks, three pairs of pants—like fatigues, only glamorous in a way. We filled out forms, stood in line for a cursory physical examination, submitted to an EKG, blood tests, and urine samples.

He recalled an internship interview in upstate New York where the intern assigned to show him around had sewn colorful piping along the seams of his white pants. It had been a sixties-style statement that was cautiously avant-garde, just enough to send a message. His sartorial statement had said, *I am hip, even if I look like an establishment square in my ice-cream-man uniform.* The poor guy had otherwise been disheveled and looked very tired, but had seemed relieved to have an hour's reprieve from another grueling day. The conversation had been somewhat stiff.

They'd walked through the ICU, the ER, the wards. He'd mentioned regular conferences and the weekly Medical Grand Rounds—the most important session, attended by all the faculty, medical residents, interns, and students. Mostly he commented about not having time to attend any of the lectures. The work was endless—spinal taps, blood-drawing, chasing down X-ray results, always interrupted by calls about a new patient being sent up from the ER to the medical floor for immediate attention. The intern had had a veneer of friendliness and ease, but it had scarcely concealed the exhaustion behind his eyes.

Most memorable: Here is the cafeteria. You won't have much time to enjoy it except to grab coffee in the middle of the night.

Today really did seem like a strange boot camp, not a celebratory welcome to internship. Luke chided himself about the analogy. He thought about his draft status. It was the same for all of his fellow medical interns. Their friends had long since been drafted; many had gone to Vietnam. Most had returned, some with memories that would haunt them forever. Others had not come back.

We, the chosen few, were declared exempt from the draft for one more year because, after four years of college and four more of medical school, we were still useless to the military. We had one more year—a training ground called the internship.

Luke thought of his own appearance. He had carried his sixties rebelliousness to medical school. It had been a tempestuous time—questioning authority had become acceptable. Audacious, often naïve calls to overthrow a broken political system had been tolerated, within limits. Looking back, he began to feel that his contribution to the rebellion as a medical student had been to dare his teachers, the nursing staff, even the patients he practiced on, to criticize his appearance.

Like a lot of others slouched in their seats in the front rows of this hospital auditorium, he assumed an individual right to wear his hair long and grow a moustache, more Fu Manchu than Clark Gable. Maybe more like Yosemite Sam. After all, like his other medical-school classmates, he had studied to exhaustion, stayed up late and arose early with his brain crying out for more sleep, going back to the hospital with never a break. He'd worried constantly about patients whose blood pressure fell to the floor, watched heart monitors display ventricular fibrillation, pounded on chests to bring back cardiac rhythm and life.

In his mind he was still a kid, barely out of college, marched into a pipeline that led in only one direction. He became part of a medical team while his friends were studying history, watching TV, planning their next pub crawl. He had been thrust into a world in which he had to grow up quickly—though in his mind, not as quickly as those who were fed into the war machine in Vietnam. At some level he felt that his high-stress world inferred certain rights, like whether or not to grow facial hair and to stick it in the eye of his professors. He was a medical student in the Age of Aquarius.

A wave of humility washed over Luke as it dawned on him that everyone in that auditorium had been given a pass. The patients he'd cared for as a medical student had not seen him as some young punk. To them he may have looked young, but all they really cared about was a reprieve from their pneumonia, heart failure, or worse. For them he need not have raised a defiant fist, railing against the system. Everyone in that drafty auditorium must have felt the same way.

His patients surely saw through the façade. They only cared that he was their doctor, albeit a student doctor. He represented hope for relief from their suffering, assurance, and the promise that they would live to see another day. In a way, he had reason to be thankful that these angelic, trusting people looked to him to be their savior. His rebellion suddenly seemed trivial. He felt embarrassed at his hubris.

He eyed the other newly minted interns surreptitiously. It was quite a mix. Some had adopted a professional hippie look similar to his. Others looked like most of his former classmates, clothed in an image that easily distinguished medical students from other graduate students. He had been quietly disdainful of their phenotypic lack of individuality. It was almost as though the way they carried themselves was an extension of the formal path they had taken to medical school. When asked, they said they were in pre-med—part of the club. They took quantitative analysis and organic chemistry, and groomed their reflection in the mirror according to a perceived idea of what a medical student should look like: scrupulously neat, short hair, clean-shaven, and always raptly attentive. Many of them appeared time-warped and were likely oblivious to the upheaval on campuses that had convulsed with teaching-assistant strikes, antiwar rallies, and welfare-rights marches.

To him, however, medical school had been almost a distraction at times. Important social issues had become the focus, such as demonstrations to support the Palestinians. Really? What had he ever known about Palestinians, except that he had wanted to be with his girlfriend, and she insisted he attend the rally? There had been picket lines to protest against Dow Chemical, the manufacturer of napalm, and sit-ins at the university administration building to protest the Kent State killings.

He recalled standing in front of his class one afternoon before the lecture began. He'd been a campus activist on a mission to improve society. Full of the energy of change, he'd stood in front of the amphitheater just before another boring pharmacology lecture.

Excuse me, can I have your attention? He'd practically shouted into the microphone.

Hey everyone, as you probably know, there's a teaching-assistant strike across the campus. They are asking everyone to support their strike and boycott class! How many are in favor?

His classmates had looked at him blankly and

said nothing. He'd persisted.

How many are opposed?

No response. Cynically, he'd continued.

How many don't care?

No response. The silence spoke volumes.

Luke shifted in his chair and shook himself from daydreams of his medical-school days. He looked around the auditorium now and wondered about these strangers sitting with him, his fellow new interns. They looked smart, maybe because he felt all his accrued medical knowledge had drained out of him. Were they like the apathetic students he knew? Who were these people? All he knew of them was from a Xeroxed photo. It was one page with twenty mug shots arranged in alphabetical order, along with the names of their medical schools: Iowa City, Berkeley, Chicago, Pittsburgh, Boston. *We have all been thrown together by some karmic coin toss*, he thought. *Whoever we may be, we will all eat, sleep, and share the same fears together, starting tomorrow.*

But even as he thought that, he wondered whether the others were as scared as he was. How much hands-on experience did they all have? Had they taken out an appendix or put in a chest tube? He began to panic inside. He should have taken more emergency-room elective time. He tried to recall the dosage of procainamide for treatment of atrial flutter.

Medical education had been so inconsistent.

He could not know whether he was ready to be a doctor. Did these strange faces know more than he did about diabetes or heart failure? What if he were alone and had to figure out how much insulin to give a diabetic child in coma? A mistake could kill the kid.

Here we all sit, an assortment of twenty-five-year-olds. We are no longer student observers. Beginning tomorrow we will have to assume the task of saying to husbands and wives and mothers that their family member has cancer, or has just died in our arms in a sea of blood and vomit. We are now the ones who will tell the families, weak-kneed and crying in pain, that their loved one is dead. How will we say it without sounding coldly clinical? . . . I'm so sorry. We did all we could . . . While thinking, Now can I be dismissed to go answer a page from the ICU? . . . As they stand shaking with grief. There's nothing more I can offer here. My job is trying to keep patients alive.

Luke knew that death meant failure. The goal was to maintain life at all costs. When a patient hung by a thread above the abyss of death, we were to step up our efforts. We would refer to our ministrations as *heroic measures*.

Thoughts of Vietnam came to him: of death and dying. Not just dying, but killing. Taking the life of a human being. How different it must be to shoot back in self-defense, or to seek out an enemy and kill him so that he won't kill you.

But any of us could kill an innocent person by making a mistake, a patient who trusted us. One wrong order, too much digoxin or insulin. Dead. No return. No do-over.

For them, it would not be to shoot or be shot. They would have to make conscious decisions based on what they know. If they were wrong, the patient would die. It must be harder to actively kill.

In our case, there is no war in which killing is sanctioned, justified. For us, it will be remembered as an indelible mistake, unforgiven and unforgotten. Thou shalt not kill. Thou shalt not even allow death to happen is what we were taught, more by example than by dictate.

Luke's thoughts wandered back two years to his first clinical rotation in medical school.

(Medical School)

One late autumn evening his teaching resident asked, Have you ever done a spinal tap? No? Well, here's your big chance.

Nightfall, and the cold had found its way through the drafty windowsill. There were four beds in the room, separated by curtains. The room was at the end of the hall on Floor 7B. Aides would deliver trays of largely inedible food in a short while.

He spent a painful hour with his new patient, meticulously documenting every detail. The guy was big, disheveled, and belligerent. Luke pulled the curtain around him, introduced himself, and began the examination with the standard question.

What brought you to the hospital?

A car, whatdja think brought me here?

This would not be easy. He tried again. What do you think is wrong?

You tell me. If I knew, I wouldn't be here.

He muddled through the exam, fumbling with his stethoscope and reflex hammer. He plunged ahead while the patient scoffed at his ineptness.

Hey, are you a doctor or an intern?

Admitting he was neither would open him to further indignity. Saying *I am a medical student* would have sounded like *I am* just *a medical student*. He might as well have said he was a history student or a janitor for the puzzled looks he'd gotten in the past.

This time he was ready—he had crafted a face-saving yet accurate answer. Interns are doctors.

He was ready also to launch into an explanation so puzzling to patients that it would stop the line of questioning. He had discovered through practice that there was enough confusion to go around, and the conversation was soon off on another tangent.

The examination nearly depleted him. Then the intern and resident coached him on the spinal tap.

OK. Roll him on his side.

He addressed the patient.

Sir, tuck your knees up.

They'd positioned Luke on a chair facing the patient's back.

OK, now feel for a space between the L4 and L5 vertebrae. Clean it with iodine. Numb the skin with lidocaine. Now take the spinal needle and direct it somewhat cephalad. Ease it in about three inches. You should feel a pop when it penetrates the dura. OK, good. Now withdraw the inner needle.

Oh, my God! There it was—clear spinal fluid, dripping like a faucet. His hands shook as he collected the fluid into three test tubes, feeling exhilarated.

But the fluid was flowing too fast.

The resident said, Oh, Christ. It's under pressure. Get the needle out now. He's *coning!*

The man's constant wisecracks and comments stopped abruptly.

The intern ran to the phone and stat-paged a neurosurgeon, who said the patient probably had a tumor pressing the brain down.

Luke remembered the anatomic description. The brain is confined in the skull, surrounded by spinal fluid that acts as a shock absorber. He recalled the neuropathologist coolly describing what happens when the fluid is released from below. The brain is pulled down by gravity, and the brain stem that controls breathing and blood pressure gets compressed at the base of the skull, like being pushed into a narrowing cone. Death occurs within minutes if surgical decompression is not performed. When he had heard it in a lecture, the whole topic seemed so abstract. Now his patient was dying.

The intern pleaded for help from the neuro-surgeon.

Luke felt like his blood pressure had plummeted to zero. His elation at succeeding at his first spinal tap flipped to barely controlled terror.

What if this guy dies? How do I explain to his wife that I caused his death? What do I do now?

The resident was calm. He told him to sit and wait. Luke replayed each moment in his head over and over, in a continuous loop. He wanted to cry but could not … better not. The patient was wheeled into the operating room. Luke waited outside the door. Two hours passed like an eternity.

The neurosurgeon pushed through the doors and pulled off his mask. He stared directly at Luke and spoke sternly and slowly for effect.

Next time, check the eyes for papilledema. If you see the optic nerve bulging, you know the intracranial pressure is increased to a dangerous level. What the hell were you thinking? Didn't you learn anything? It's the only way to know if it's safe to do an LP when you suspect increased pressure. Your patient damn near died.

The surgeon had paused and quieted down. He'll be OK. We removed a frontal lobe meningioma and decompressed the brain. I hope you learned a lesson.

It was not the last lesson. Three months later a different resident told him to do a bone marrow aspiration on an elderly woman.

You've seen enough of them—go do it.

Then he was alone with a nurse and the patient. She unwrapped the sterile blue cloth that covered the bone marrow tray. The patient lay flat on her back, bare-chested. She was discreetly covered except for her sternum. He felt for the bony landmarks, the xiphoid process, the ribs that articulated with the sternum, easy to see and feel on this skinny lady. Then he put on the sterile gloves, trying to exude nonchalance. He couldn't help but think of how barbaric the procedure was. Numb the skin with lidocaine, down to the bone. Make a small stab wound. Insert the trocar, the size of a fat nail. Screw it into the sternum. Attach a syringe. Suck out the marrow with a quick pull. The final step invariably caused the patient to cry out in agony. They were never forewarned about the intensity of the pain. To do so would only intensify their anxiety. It only lasted a second. The syringe would fill with thick, bloody bone marrow fluid. Then quickly pull out the trocar. As he snapped off the latex gloves, he would say, *OK. We're done.* The patient would look up, wide awake, terrified, and then sigh with relief that the torture was over. He would wheel around and stride from the room. He replayed the scenario in his head.

Then he began. The trocar went in too easily. It was as if the breastbone was mushy, like he was penetrating an eggshell. The patient got pale and started breathing fast. She cried out.

My chest hurts. Help me. I can't breathe.

Luke remembered thinking, I must have missed the sternum. Oh my god, maybe I stuck the lung or the pericardium. She could die.

He calmly told the nurse to call the resident as he stood stoically over the patient and stared at the drops of blood oozing from the puncture site. The nurse called the resident. He looked up at the seconds ticking on the wall clock. Time slowed to a stop. Jesus. Please hurry. He was powerless, standing at the bedside, holding the patient's hand.

You'll be OK, he told her, hoping it was not a lie.

The resident had charged in.

Get me an EKG machine. Luke, go stand outside. I'll take over. We need to make sure she does not have pericardial tamponade. Order a stat X-ray to check for pneumothorax.

Luke had stood out in the hall. He remembered the room, the mauve walls, the exact position where he had stood. He remembered thinking about the pericardial sac filling up with blood so the heart couldn't beat. The panic he had felt thinking of her dying because of an error he had made was indelibly inscribed in his brain. He thought, *if she dies I will leave medical school. I couldn't live with myself. Killing an elderly lady because of a stupid mistake.*

The resident came out.

It's OK. No electrical alternans on the EKG, so no pericardial bleeding. She has a small pneumothorax. The lung collapse you created with the needle puncture isn't severe. No need for a chest tube. It'll re-expand on its own. She has a very narrow sternum, so I'm not surprised you missed it. You have to be very careful.

His reassurance had been unforgettable; this resident physician who'd always carried a ballpoint pen behind his ear and never showed the slightest lack of confidence. Luke would always think of him as his angel.

Then he thought of his first surgical rotation. There he was in the hospital cafeteria line, at six a.m., dressed in a tie and short white coat, waiting for a dollop of lukewarm, scrambled eggs while the crazy, bastard chief resident pummeled him with questions.

So, hotshot, what are the major nerves that innervate the bladder and what is their function?

Always more questions, more intimidation. He had thought, *This guy is nuts.*

The resident was talking to him and a fellow student.

You guys are lazy slugs. You will never be surgeons.

OK, Luke got it. He wasn't a surgeon and likely would never choose to be. Why had he been required to study all night, then stand across an operating table holding retractors before most people had been awake, and field insults between surgeries?

(Internship)

Back at the internship orientation, a short, stern-looking man with a hawk-like nose interrupted Luke's reverie by striding into the auditorium. His neatly combed gray hair was parted down the middle. He wore a buttoned, starched white coat. The Chief of Medicine. He stopped in the middle of the stage, his lips tight. Despite his fierce demeanor, he somehow looked kindly. He wore a stethoscope prominently draped down his chest. The symbolic medical tie had never looked better on any doctor Luke had seen.

Good morning, ladies and gentlemen.

He looked over the group, his face serious, and made eye contact with each one.

I want to welcome you to Providence on your first day as new doctors.

He paused. Starting today and for the rest of your life, you will be known to the world as *Doctor.*

Never forget the privilege, the honor, and the responsibility that go with the title. You have arrived at a point in your career where you join a very special profession that dates back to Hippocrates. Never forget that. The next year of your life will be the best year or the worst.

Every word was measured.

You will work long hours, night and day. You will see sickness that you have never seen before. You will experience highs and lows you never dreamed imaginable. You will feel at times that you know nothing, that you are inadequate for the job. But when the year is over, you will look back with astonishment at how much you have learned. Look around this room. You twenty young men and women have been handpicked from across the country as the brightest and most capable out of thousands of graduating medical students. You are a team. We are proud to have you here and will do our best to make this the most rewarding experience of your life. Welcome.

With that, he was gone. The twenty sat mute, then slowly trickled out. Luke looked at his schedule. Tomorrow morning at eight, he was due in the ER for the twelve-hour day shift, his first day as a doctor.

Chapter 3

January 1987 (Medical Practice — Year Ten)

A phone call from the ER woke Luke from a deep sleep. The voice on the other end spoke. We have an elderly gentleman here. His name is Walter Curry. He says you are his doctor.

Yes. What's going on?

He was brought in by ambulance. He's on a stretcher, conscious and alert, though he kinda mumbles when he talks. Vital signs are stable. We're running oxygen at 2 liters and an IV with D5W ½ normal saline at 75 cc. His O2 sat is 89.

It took a minute to come out of his sleep fog. Then it sank in. Walter, his dear old friend, was dying. His life had funneled down to a few mundane details recited robotically by the ER doctor. Who could fault him? He was simply trying to unload a burden at three a.m. so he could attend to assorted denizens of the night who awaited him behind closed drapes — an endless stream of medical complaints, drunkenness, car accidents. It was called triage. One less patient to deal with. Just business as usual.

OK. I'll be right there.

An uncharacteristically icy blast greeted him as he stepped out of the mudroom of their log home and into the blackness. The old diesel pickup coughed to a start and sputtered along the lane to the gate. Its familiar rattle offered some comfort in the still, freezing night. The headlights followed the sandy ruts past the warped, three-board fence as the truck creaked and moaned over the quarter mile to the gate.

Luke stopped, undid the chain, exited, stopped, relocked the chain, then turned onto the gravel road and pushed in the choke. The steps had become rote, the same drill for ten long years. He drove along the road sheltered by a canopy of live oaks, past the fire tower on the right side, silhouetted by a full moon. Then it was down the hill to the main road and ten miles straight across the prairie. The truck practically drove itself.

No lights, no cars—just the prairie grass illuminated by his headlights, stiff and motionless, in the frigid predawn of New Year's Day. It was a time to think. About what? That January 1 is a day to sleep late, or once had been for him, so many years ago? That it was the first day of his tenth year of medical practice? A decade ago he'd thought the rhythmic thrill of being a doctor would last forever.

But this day—cold, dark, and lonely—matched his mood. He knew the weather would warm up, then freeze again, the cycle repeating itself until spring. For him the cycle had become the same. This year, he hoped the spring thaw would work its magic on his brain like it did on the world outside.

Luke's thoughts drifted back to Walter, an enigmatic old man who lived alone and barely spoke. He was always moving his hands, and he stuttered nervously when he talked. His shock of white hair and bushy white moustache drew an obvious, endearing comparison. His eyes even twinkled and lit up his shy smile. He spoke with his camera when words would not work for him. He would offer a beefy finger to the little kids as he walked them around the church playground with his Nikon hanging around his neck, always ready for an interesting photo. All anyone knew about him was that he was a retired engineer from Detroit, and that he had a son somewhere.

Luke parked the truck and buzzed himself into the back corridor of the hospital. He strode down the fluorescent-lit empty hall to the ER. The ER doctor in his wrinkled scrubs slouched on a stool, talking on the phone. He looked haggard. He pointed down the hall. A nurse said, Room Six. She handed him a clipboard.

Walter was alone behind the curtain, a blanket pulled to his chin. A green oxygen line had been fastened around his face, the short cannula running up into his nose. His formerly ruddy cheeks had become deeply jaundiced and looked green in the fluorescent light. An intravenous line snaked out from under the blanket. The heart monitor beeped unevenly with his pulse, asynchronous with his labored, grunting breaths.

Hello, Walter.

Halloo. His weak, sonorous voice somehow generated a sound from the depths.

You hurting?

Not so bad.

In your stomach?

Uh-huh.

I'll give you something for the pain.

Uh-huh.

Luke touched his shoulder.

I'll get you upstairs. Anything else I can do?

Uh-uh.

He wrote the perfunctory orders: admit to hospital, diagnosis pancreatic cancer, condition terminal, pain medications, diet, oxygen, DNR—do not resuscitate. He hesitated as he wrote the last, but Walter's time had come.

Luke stifled a hitch in his breath, an aborted sob. He felt sad, but pushed the feeling back. He recalled those lazy Sunday afternoons when he and his young daughter had visited Walter. The old guy had loved Lucy like a precious granddaughter. He had never seemed happier than when he could spend an afternoon with her, snapping pictures

with his omnipresent camera. One day, he'd captured her so perfectly, a two-year-old sitting with
her toys, wearing a little T-shirt with Humpty
Dumpty on the front, and looking up at him with
her coal-black eyes.

The image lingered in Luke's mind as he left
the room. What good was he now, except to ease
Walter's departure from the world? He thought of
Dylan Thomas's words as he famously beseeched
his father in his poem, *Do Not Go Gentle into that
Good Night*, to rage against the dying of the light.

The burning fire of Walter's life was gone. No
rage could bring it back. Luke no longer clung to
the long-abandoned tenet that his job was to
maintain life at all costs. He had failed in that quix-
otic pursuit so many times that he had finally
grown to accept that all life came to an end, which
he was often powerless even to delay. What had
driven him in the past to believe that life was
sacred? Those words imply that death is the anti-
thesis, an abhorrent failure to keep the candle
burning. Over many painful years, he had come to
realize that existence—birth, life, and death—is an
immutable continuum. Sometimes he could stretch
it out, but he could not control its eventual end.

He forced his thoughts away and decided to
see his other patients while he was there.

What the hell, he thought. It's a little early but I
might as well get a jump on the day.

He awakened them one by one. Groggy-eyed,

they looked at him like some unwelcome specter. He checked their lungs and heart, then left them wondering whether it was a dream. He scribbled notes in their charts with various orders and shuffled out the door into the morning light.

He arrived home, his presence announced by the small bell at the back door. Betsy was standing at the kitchen sink.

Hi, honey. He paused to steady his voice.

Got some bad news. Walter's dying.

The words left a lump in his throat and he looked away.

She looked at him, stunned, and put her hands down. She barely suppressed her tears, like him, thinking of the dear old guy lying alone as he waited for the end. Now three and a half, Lucy sat watching TV in the next room, oblivious.

The following day, the first Monday of the new year, he rushed through hospital rounds knowing he would have an office full of patients. It was as though everyone had a pent-up New Year's resolution to go to the doctor before lapsing into their bad habits for the rest of the year. He stopped by Walter's room. It was too late to say good-bye. He was in a coma. There was no more to do. A wave of grief swept over Luke, then receded as fast as it had come, displaced by thoughts of the hectic day he faced.

Back in his office, he went from one room to the next seeing patients with sore throats, high blood pressure, back pain, heart failure. His care was methodical, if not mechanical. They did not seem to notice. Toward the end of the morning, Tammie, Luke's office nurse, pulled him aside.

She was crying. Walter's dead.

He hurried across the street to the hospital and walked into Walter's room. No one was at the bed-side. A crisp white sheet was folded neatly at his neck. His eyes and mouth were closed. There was no movement, no life. He ritualistically listened for heart sounds and heard none. He stood there for a moment and marveled, once again, at how death was like flipping off a switch. On, then off. It was that blunt. No matter how close to the end, a living being was light years different from a corpse, he thought. Walter was no longer a person. The dichotomy was so striking it was no wonder that people believed in a soul that carried life some-where else.

He said good-bye but did not know why. Per-haps the words came out to gain closure in his own mind, like a period at the end of a sentence. He completed the death certificate and returned to the office for an afternoon as busy as the morning.

One week later he admitted John Greer to the hospital. It had been two years, he recalled, since he'd first met the Reverend John. He had helped recruit him to be the new minister for their church. The church was nondenominational and suited Luke. He had no use for rigid dogma. The furthest he got away from science to explain the existence of life on earth was his effort to blend art and science in the practice of medicine. The theological argument to explain where we come from and why we are here invariably ends with a single word—faith. To him it was ludicrous to end the teleological debate by declaring that belief—even a widely held belief—is truth. To his mind, truth must be measurable. Otherwise, it is speculation spun into an allegory—at best, a fairy tale.

Nevertheless, for him, those Sunday mornings with his family provided a real, if brief respite from the professional life that had begun to close in around him. He felt at times like a piece of driftwood propelled helter-skelter down a narrowing flume.

Several months ago John had taken him aside asking whether he would be his doctor. At the time he'd been amused to think he'd be ministering to the minister. Before long it had become clear that the night sweats and weight loss were serious. John had a lymphoma that had spread into his bone marrow and throughout his lymphatic system. He'd denied his symptoms until it was too late.

John had begged, Please don't tell my parishioners. I knew something was wrong a few months after I was hired.

After that, Sunday mornings became different. Luke no longer had an escape from his total immersion in sickness. He looked up and saw his minister's biological clock ticking down as he stood in the pulpit, a secret shared with no one in the congregation but him. His tiny, Sunday morning window of respite from death and dying had closed.

Luke understood. John was only human. Yes, even a minister. No one escapes being human. He needed health insurance and a job. Maybe he'd deluded himself into believing that his cancer would go away. Every Sunday he preached hope and trust and forgiveness. Over coffee after the service one day, Luke was sharing in small talk with church members.

Reverend John's a great guy, they said. We're glad he's here.

Yes, he's a good guy.

But Luke recalled an evening a few months before at a quiet social dinner with several couples from the church and the minister. As the group sat around the room with their drinks, making idle conversation, John, in a socially clumsy move, revealed that one of the guests—a particularly frail woman, who had mistakenly thought she was attending a harmless dinner party—had a serious anxiety problem.

Martha, you're among friends. Do you want to share your issues?

He persisted with his armchair psychology until she broke down in humiliation, as if she were undergoing an exorcism. The others in the room remained silent, uncomfortable bystanders. Luke saw hypocrisy in this man who would not share his own weaknesses but could drag another poor soul through the mud. He held his tongue, though he was sorely tempted to expose John's insensitivity. *Can't he see how Martha is suffering?*

Luke thought about that incident as he drove to the hospital. The pain of facing mortality in silence drives people to act in strange ways. Even ministers are human.

John lay in bed, pale and weak. He looked up with sunken, pleading eyes.

I don't think I'm going to make it, he croaked.

Luke took his hand and stood silent in the quiet room. John's expression had a hopeless, frightened look that was all too familiar—eyes that said, *It's the end.* There was no need to speak.

I'll make sure you're comfortable, John, and I'll be back later.

He bowed his head and backed slowly out of the room, scratched a few notes in the chart, then left. He felt strangely unemotional. *Another death, another friend gone. Mercifully,* he thought, *it's over.*

He chastised himself at his inability to conjure up even a wave of sadness, a tear, any feeling at all after saying goodbye for the last time. *What is happening to me? I do care. I do my best.*

Once again, the life candle was blown out. Only wisps of memory, like smoke, remained to slowly dissipate. No more, no less. His thoughts about John were deadened by the endless, relentless rhythm of seeing other patients all day long, room after room, ward after ward.

Sometime later, at a cocktail party, an acquaintance cornered him and asked, How do you do it? You take care of sick people day after day. You watch your patients die. I barely know anyone with cancer. You see them all the time. I sell insurance; it's pretty boring but I don't have to stare death in the face every day.

He shrugged.

It's my job.

But he knew it was not just a job like any other. The insurance salesman was right. All he saw was sickness and death—at the grocery store, at a party, at his office, all week long, year in, year out. Each dying patient added an increasingly intolerable weight, and suppressing his feelings became more difficult by the day. He had created a wall over the years. On the surface it was just a job. But behind the wall, he labored under a burden he could not share. Saying good-bye to friends as they passed away, one after another. Nothing left but an obituary and a memory that did not linger for long. Was he subconsciously afraid that opening up a seam would release an ocean of tears being held back? He couldn't take that chance. He would not conjure up a tear.

Chapter 4

January 1973 (Internship)

The interns' on-call room was small. It reminded Luke of an austere cell in a Trappist monastery where he'd spent a weekend at a retreat imposed on him and his high school classmates. He thought back. Why would the nuns subject him and his testosterone-fueled pals to such an experience? They would have said to enhance spirituality. It had been memorable only for its abject dreariness.

He recalled a tour through the dorm where the monks slept in plywood cubicles, completely open on one side. He and his friends had lifted the paper-thin mattresses and uncovered small whips that were used for self-flagellation. On the foot of one bed was a neatly folded army blanket. He was mystified as to who would choose a cloistered life of total isolation. The worn blanket told the story. At least some of the monks entered the monastery after suffering shell shock during World War II and had been there for decades. They had simply given up on all attempts to adjust to life after the horrors of war.

Burned out, they had checked out, and entered a world of regimentation where the only words spoken were prayers and chanting. Somehow for them, simply being alive was enough. He had sat behind a screen and listened as the monks chanted their Matins and Lauds in Latin, long before dawn in a cold, dim chapel, and he had thought about the choice they had made. Their haunting voices still echoed in his mind. He thought of those long-forgotten men and the claustrophobic cell where he had spent that endless weekend.

Here he was again. The interns' room had a single bed along the wall. A small desk stood next to the bed beneath a window covered by twisted white venetian blinds, bent in random places. The window shook with the wind in the early January twilight, and the freezing cold permeated the room. The desk was littered with papers, journals, and books from previous transient occupants. A half-empty Styrofoam coffee cup stood abandoned, the only testimony to a sudden call for some unknown emergency. He could not bear to turn on the single overhead light. Only the dimmed hall lights intruded into the gloom.

An early evening on a winter Sunday found him trapped in this desolate room as the only doctor on the pediatric unit, waiting for the shock of his pager to call him to the next crisis. What it would be was anyone's guess. He knew only that it would come. He lay on the bed, propped against a pillow, rumpled sheets underneath, a bed never made properly because its inhabitants never slept. He tried to read, to cram a few more medical facts into his brain, but was paralyzed by a toxic mixture of stress and inertia. He stared past the open door and listened halfheartedly to the sound of an occasional footstep far down the hall.

His thoughts meandered, each one seeming to drag him deeper into the depths of loneliness. Tonight, whatever glamour had been immortalized in the heroic television exploits of Dr. Kildare was as distant to him as a black hole. He lay there alone, unable to read or eat or sleep, waiting for his pager to startle him back to reality.

A few hours before, as the cold day faded into night, he had answered a phone call. It was his wife. She got straight to the point. There was no patter— like, *How's it going,* or *Hope you're not too busy.*

Her voice was businesslike.

I know you will be in the hospital until tomorrow night. I just wanted to tell you I'm having dinner with a guy from my office.

Why are you telling me that?

Just thought you should know.

Her unspoken message was clear. The brief conversation ended as it began. He knew his young marriage had been a false start and was fading away, but the pain of abandonment and loneliness was stifling. He thought about his life, their life. He was alone in his own damned monastic cell—no energy, no appetite.

The adrenaline rush he felt as an intern was a positive addiction, but like any addict he paid a price for it. Their short-lived marriage was a candle flickering out—neither of them wished to relight it. Nonetheless, he felt a sense of helplessness.

He tried to analyze it objectively, dispassionately, as if to wallow in it would help him cope. He slipped in and out of self-pity. Then his pager buzzed.

The nurse was frantic.

Doctor James, you have a new patient. She is fifteen years old, sent up from the ER. We just wheeled her into three sixty-seven. You'd better come stat. She's confused and screaming and thrashing all over the place. Almost broke the restraints. Pulled out the IV.

His throat was dry as cotton and his heart pounded away as he sprinted down the hall. He entered the room and stopped. Before him was a teenage girl, tugging desperately against restraints that held her onto the bed, delirious, screaming in terror, with mucous running from her mouth. She looked grotesque. Her skin was deeply jaundiced and her jet-black hair was matted against her forehead. Her eyes were wild, insane.

The panicked nurse blurted out a few words.

They called from the ER and said they had a

girl with high fever and confusion. We had no idea she was like this. She started going crazy in the elevator on the way up here.

Her voice was quaking but she was visibly relieved that he was there, thankful that someone else could bear the burden of making the decisions, standing by for orders to occupy her, to allow her to switch into mechanical mode. Any task, just name it. Anything at all to distract her from this girl who had become a feral animal. Her continuous screaming echoed around the small room. The nurse wanted to run, to cover her ears—anything to escape. She had likely never heard a human being emit such a sound.

Luke did not hesitate because he could not. The distraught nurse displayed what he felt, but his training had taught him to take charge. He spoke in a calm voice, quiet but direct.

Give her five milligrams of Valium. Get her chart. What are her vitals? Did they do any labs? Let's get that IV restarted and run it with dextrose and saline at 125 cc. Check those restraints. Raise the bed to thirty degrees. Close the door. Get me a subclavian tray. Oxygen at four liters.

The orders rolled from his mouth. He only raised his voice to be heard above the screaming. The terrified girl looked as though she was being tortured mercilessly. Two or three nurses ran to follow his directions. The fear in their eyes gave way to their training.

He quickly established that she would not die of a cardiac arrest. The screaming stopped as she faded into a stupor as the sedative took effect. He prepped the skin under her clavicle and passed a large bore needle into the subclavian vein. Then he threaded a catheter over the needle, withdrew the needle and attached the catheter to the intravenous line. He sewed the catheter to the skin and snapped off the latex gloves.

He had a quiet interval to look at all the lab tests and try to piece together a diagnosis. An hour passed. Then two, three more flew by like minutes. Lab tests came trickling back. She had hemolytic anemia—something was destroying her red blood cells. Tests of her liver and kidney function looked like those vital organs had exploded. She slept fitfully in her delirium. Her temperature was 104°F, even when covered by a cooling blanket. She was in total physical collapse. Heavy sedation gave way at intervals to blood-curdling screams.

Luke was alone with her now, nearing midnight, unwilling to leave her bedside until he figured out a diagnosis. He could sedate her and stop the screaming, but that was not enough. She could be dead very soon if he didn't have an answer. He sat next to her bed and reviewed her chart. Maria Gonsalves. The floor was littered with the detritus of a resuscitation: syringes, tape, gauze, bloody towels, needle covers.

She took long, deep, sighing breaths. Her dark

hair was still matted against her sweaty forehead. Beneath the otherworldly glow of jaundice, he could see she was a beautiful young girl. He put his stethoscope on her chest. Suddenly her mania erupted and she bolted upright, screaming. He backed away and pushed more sedative into her IV. She faded out. But when he touched her skin, she awakened again, shrieking so loud his ears hurt. Her skin was so sensitive that one brief touch would set her off.

Her parents came down the hall and stood outside the room, shaking, crying, trying to console each other. He tried to remain coolly professional, barely hiding his own fear and confusion. He knew they needed to believe in someone. Prayers were an abstraction. They wanted help for their daughter. He began what seemed like a gentle interrogation.

When did she get sick?

How did it start?

What did you notice first?

Then what? Where do you live?

Anyone else in the family sick?

Does she have any ongoing illnesses?

Any pets?

He pummeled them with questions. Their answers were disjointed and interrupted with sobs and pleas to save her. They spoke in heavily accented English, despite having emigrated from the Azores decades before.

Oh, Doctor. You've got to help her. She's our

only child. Oh my God, our Maria. Please, Doctor.

We're doing everything we can. Please try to get some rest. I will be with her all night. I'll come to see you later.

He watched them huddle together and shuffle away to the waiting room for an all-night vigil. They were simply dressed, confused, weeping. Powerless.

He walked back into the room. Now it was past midnight.

Goddamn it. Don't die on me, Maria, he muttered.

He rechecked her blood pressure. It was low, but unchanged. Her skin was on fire. He reviewed what he knew: high fever, jaundice, shock, bleeding, kidney and liver failure. He racked his brain. He pored through a medical book, trying to come up with a diagnosis. He had never seen anything like this.

What did he know? She lived on a farm, had a pet dog, had gotten a fever and aches a day or two ago. It was obvious she had an overwhelming infection. He went through a litany of possibilities, then boiled it down to the most feasible one. Could she have fulminant leptospirosis? Everything seemed to fit. But he needed to see a blood smear under a special dark field microscope. He had a brief reservation about calling the hospital microbiologist at home in the dead of night. But the girl's need won out. He called and identified himself, related the story in a brief, organized, logical way.

The microbiologist barely paused.

I'll be right there. Get a fresh tube of blood and meet me in the micro lab.

Luke hung up the phone, grateful beyond words.

They pored over the blood specimen under the microscope. They saw red blood cells that looked like irregular boulders at high magnification.

Jesus, take a look at this. These look like spirochetes teeming in the blood stream. They're spinning through the plasma. It's bizarre. It's like they're taking over her body. The inoculum is overwhelming!

The huge lab was normally filled with lab techs during the day. On this cold winter night, it was ghostly; the only light was on the table where they were working. Luke hunched over the microscope. He saw the spinning, twisting bacterial forms interspersed between red blood cells. It was a horrible, frightening sight. If he could actually see them, the concentration of bacteria in her body had to be immeasurably huge. He had a diagnosis; now he needed to try to keep her alive. How could it be that these strange microorganisms could appear in such overwhelming numbers? He shivered at the thought.

He ran back and increased the penicillin dose.

Exhaustion lowered a curtain of sleep as Luke sat at her bedside. He awakened suddenly, his brain exploding with emotions. Her blood pressure had fallen. He gave her intravenous stimulants to raise it. He called for units of blood. She was bleeding now from her nose and mouth. Her eyes opened with a panicked look that penetrated through him, begging to know what was happening to her. He felt her wordless pleading, as if she were drowning and raising her arm for help. Then she sank back into a fitful repose.

The hours ticked by as he stood next to her, or sat at the bedside. His eyes were scratchy with tiredness; his body demanding sleep. He watched her uneven breathing, and dreaded her frequent wakening into deafening, bloodcurdling sounds as she fought against her arm and chest restraints. Morning came. A new shift of nurses arrived. She seemed to be sleeping, heavily sedated with narcotics. All day he stopped by her room between managing other patients. There had been no time for a shower or change of clothes.

His shift ended in the evening and he drove home. The blinking answering machine beckoned in the shade-drawn room. The message was from his wife.

Call me. We need to talk.

He was numb by then, turned off the machine, muttered, No more talk, then passed out on his bed. His marriage was crumbling and all he could think of was sleep.

The next day he was back at the hospital.

Maria's jaundice had deepened. Her appearance nearly choked him up.

He spoke to her parents. Looking lost and frightened they pleaded with him.

How could this happen? She's such a good girl. She never did anything wrong. She studies hard in school and everyone loves her.

Her mother clutched Luke's arm. He stayed with them for a few minutes, and tried to reassure them.

We're doing everything we can. She has a serious infection.

He would not allow himself to say her chances of surviving became less by the hour.

Their fear and sadness had punctured his clinical armor. His words began to sound pointless, even to him, as he tried to relieve their emotional desperation. He wondered whether his words sounded as hopeless as he felt.

Maria was dying. He leafed through books and journals in the medical library looking for any clue to improve her odds. She was infected by Leptospira. The disease had found its way through her entire body and was destroying her liver and kidneys. It was in her brain. He came across a recent article that summarized a radical approach to treating patients who were dying of liver failure. The small series of patients in the report were beyond any hope of survival with conventional treatment. The authors theorized that if they could remove whatever toxin continued to damage the liver, they could reverse the inevitable death. Their idea was to anesthetize the patient and cool the body down in order to slow metabolic activity. Then the surgeon would remove all their blood and replace it with saline, then very quickly re-transfuse them with new blood. They called the procedure "total body washout."

The authors reported a better than fifty percent success rate in the patients they had treated. In Maria's case, to do nothing would mean a one hundred percent chance of death. Luke thought the idea was far-fetched, but he discussed the idea with his faculty physician, and agreed that only such an extreme approach had a chance to save her life.

Luke told her parents in as gentle a voice as he could muster. His words were honest, but tinged with hope. He walked alongside the stretcher as she was wheeled into the operating room. He donned a scrub suit and mask and stood near the operating table. They administered an anesthetic to deepen her coma, then reduced her body temperature to slow her metabolic rate. The surgeon placed a catheter the size of a small hose into her femoral artery on one side, and another into the large femoral vein on the other side. He proceeded to infuse saline through the artery and remove blood from the vein.

The blood went from red to pink. Then it became clear. She had nothing flowing through her bloodstream but saline. No oxygen-carrying hemoglobin. No white blood cells. Only the low body temperature kept her brain from dying. As soon as the blood draining from her became clear, the surgeon began to infuse fresh blood, pint after pint, until the venous blood ran red once again.

Three hours later it was done. She was wheeled to the intensive care unit, where Luke waited. She was intubated and comatose, the ventilator pulsing rhythmically to maintain her breathing. Her body had swelled as though she was blown up with air because of the massive fluid shift. *Of course*, he thought, *she would be blown up without the blood protein, albumin, to modulate the movement of fluid in and out of her tissues.* He was nonetheless shocked at her appearance. This beautiful young girl had become unrecognizable, deeply jaundiced, and bloated beyond recognition.

He added albumin and monitored her blood oxygen. He sat with her, looking for any sign that her bodily functions would come back. They did not. Within a few hours her heart rate slowed, then stopped. The monitor showed ventricular fibrillation—her heart had stopped beating. Her blood pressure fell to zero. Only the ventilator kept up its regular sound, pushing air into her lungs with no effect. She was dead.

Luke turned off the ventilator, then walked slowly to the waiting room. Her parents could read his face. They thanked him and held each other. He walked away, emotionally shot, feeling like a failure. He could only hope that the beautiful memories of their dear daughter would sustain them.

As for him, he had no one to share his grief with. He could only dream of what she might have looked like grown up, a mother with a family. He thought of the senselessness of her death. He found himself stuck with the usual clichés. Mostly he felt alone.

As the months rolled by, Luke gradually became inured to the suffering and loss of his patients and the relentless onslaught that faced him day and night. His thoughts returned to those haunting words of the medical chief on the first day of his internship. *This will be the best year of your life or the worst.*

He would make it the best. Not to commit to that would have made the long months intolerable. He would continue to make every effort to focus singularly on his patients, through the interminable hours and the haze of exhaustion. Concern for his patients would be his only mission—everything else in his life would be on hold. He knew the extremes: the highs of bringing patients with flat-line EKG's back to life. The smiles and tears of gratitude. Even the lows: saying, That's it. We can't bring the patient back. Thanks to everyone for trying.

These experiences would sustain him.

Chapter 5

New to private practice, Luke had agreed to take referrals from the emergency room, a way to begin building a patient load. None of these patients had a primary care physician, most had no insurance, and they typically only sought care when it was a dire emergency. That is how he met Levon Padgett.

Luke sat in his office one morning, sipping coffee and surrounded by his beloved medical books. *Not a bad life*, he thought, looking out his window. It faced an alley like the one behind his childhood home. What an odd memory, he mused, but one that gave him great comfort. Too bad he had to work to make a living. Drinking coffee, lost in thought, seemed like a good way to spend a day. Tammie interrupted him.

Your new patient is ready.

He donned his clean, starched white coat, pulled the chart from the rack, and opened the door to a new challenge. Levon Padgett looked up from where he slouched in his filthy bib overalls. If there is such a thing as a stereotypic redneck, Levon was the poster child.

Through the stubble on his face emerged a broad, nearly toothless grin. The stench of stale sweat mixed with his acrid tobacco breath was nearly overpowering. His arms were crossed over his fat stomach, merging with his chest into one great protuberance. He wore a grimy cap askew on his head. The logo on the front read: *If you ain't from Dothan, you ain't shit.*

Levon stuck out a fat paw.

Luke, hiding a mixture of disgust and amusement, shook Levon's hand and introduced himself.

The patient sized him up.

Hidy, Doc. Name's Levon.

The gravelly words came out as though his mouth was full of tongue and tobacco, possibly with a partial denture plate floating loose. When he began to speak, the letter 's' came out as 'sh' or 'zh,' as though he needed to keep his mouth closed so the tobacco juice wouldn't run out.

So, what can I do for you, Mr. Padgett?

Doc, I got the sugar diabetish. Sent me over from 'mergency. Said you might could regulate me. Me'n my wife live 'bout twenty miles outside of town, kinda near to Ramford. It ain't real easy gittin' here, but I come cuz I felt like my sugar was out of whack.

Luke learned that his new patient was a guard at the maximum-security state prison, and that his wife supposedly had heart trouble and was seeing another doctor.

Who's her doctor?

Hell, Doc, I don' know his name. He's over yonder, other end'a town.

The visit ended with a plan for Levon to return in a month. He rose to leave.

Say Doc, I kiney like you. I was wonderin' can my wife come 'n see you? She don't cotton much to that other doctor, and I believe she'd feel right comfortable with you.

When he left, the trail of bad odors slowly dissipated. Luke sat down in his office and wrote some notes. He had a grand total of two new patients. *This will be one hell of a practice if they're all like Levon Padgett.*

As it happened, Levon was often around to liven things up, never without fanfare, but always without warning.

One morning he barged into the office and announced that he needed to see the doctor. The waiting room was nearly full, but Tammie knew it was better to usher him into an exam room than to allow him to park himself in the waiting room and risk having the other waiting patients leave in disgust.

Luke sucked in his breath, opened the door, and greeted him.

Hey there, Levon. What brings you here so suddenly without an appointment?

Doc, I was workin' at the prizhin yesterday. I had just fed the prizhnerz and was walkin' up the stairs, takin' 'em back to their cells. I gave 'em over to another guard cuz I was feelin' dizzy. So I went and took another dose of insulin cuz I figgered it was the sugar. Nex' thing I know, I woken up in the 'firmary with some camel-jockey doc lookin' down at me. Sent me on home and said I should see you. So here I am.

Despite endless explanations about his illness, it was apparent that Levon had retained nothing. How many times had Luke told him that having diabetes meant his body did not make insulin, and insulin was essential because it helped sugar—glucose—get into the body's cells to provide energy? If he gave himself too much insulin, he would get dizzy and need to drink or eat something sugary to counteract the excess insulin.

Luke tried again, slowly.

Levon, when you felt dizzy, it was most likely that you had not eaten and you had taken too much insulin. It lowered your blood sugar too much, so you needed to eat or drink something with sugar in it. Instead, you took more insulin which made your blood sugar fall so low that you fainted.

This short lecture fell on deaf ears. Levon just didn't get it.

It seemed like that first year would be dominated by Levon Padgett.

One night, only months after he had begun his practice, the phone rang at four a.m. Hello, Doc. This is the county sheriff. We responded to a call from a Levon Padgett who claims you're his doctor. Can I put him on the line?

Then the familiar voice came through.

Hey, Doc, thish here Levon. Got bad newzh, Doc. My wife done died.

His words were garbled as usual, but the tone of his voice was completely unemotional. Then there was silence.

Wait a second. What did you just say?

My wife died.

What happened?

Don' know, Doc. She got up and went into the bathroom. Then I heard a racket. Soz I got up, and I sheen her lyin' nex' the commode. Couldn't wake her up, soz I called the Reshcue. You wanna talk to 'em?

Someone took the phone.

Hello, Doctor. This is the county coroner out here at the Padgett residence. I was called by Rescue when they found Mrs. Padgett lying on the floor in the bathroom. She was deceased. Looks like natural causes to me. It would be helpful if you agreed. Then I wouldn't have to take her back and do an autopsy.

Luke gathered his thoughts as best he could in the fog of the middle-of-the-night confusion and staccato reports from someplace twenty miles outside of town. He could picture the Rescue truck and police cars, blue-and-red lights illuminating broken-down fences and a sagging porch. He managed to dredge up her clinical history and talk to the coroner.

Yes, she was my patient. She complained about having occasional chest pains, but her cardiac workup was completely negative. She was only thirty-seven. It seems very strange that she would suddenly collapse and die. Doesn't it seem a little odd to you that a woman her age would suddenly drop dead?

There was a pause.

Look, Doc, we're way out in the country up here. I don't see anything suspicious, and it sure looks like natural causes. So, I'd appreciate it if you'd agree so we could go ahead and release the body to the funeral director.

He thought for a moment. His righteous principles slowly began to succumb to some backwoods standard completely foreign to him. He sensed impatience on the other end of the line, an unspoken message about rules of behavior with which he was unfamiliar.

Well, I guess so, if what you say is true.

The coroner said, Thanks, Doc, and hung up the phone.

Levon Padgett drifted away sometime after that episode. Luke heard a few years later that he had died of a heart attack.

Those early years were invigorating—one unique tale after another—in his office and at the hospital. It was exciting to stride through the hospital seeing his patients, and sometimes seeing other doctors' patients as a consultant in his specialty of pulmonary diseases. He couldn't help but feel a little proud when other doctors asked him to do a consult. Now and then, a patient died. But the balance stayed on the side of success stories. The hours were long, but the pay was good. He carried the weight of worry easily.

As an intern he could never imagine the notion of having another wife, much less children—a family. Through all the years of intense training his whole being was dedicated to sharpening his medical skills, hungrily gorging himself on new information, never sated. There had been no time for any but brief distractions.

After several years he began to take stock. When he met Betsy, almost at once his life path took a turn. His brief first marriage was so far in the rearview mirror, it was a distant memory, more a trial run between two impetuous young souls.

They had both come to the realization that it was a false start.

Still, the idea of marriage only brought bad feelings, even years later—until he met Betsy. Introduced at a small party, their mutual attraction was immediate. He was drawn to her deep brown eyes with long lashes and prominent eyebrows that gave her a sultry look. Her face was lightly freckled and framed by long, curly hair. Her gravitational pull overwhelmed all sights or sounds around him.

They became entwined, alike in so many ways, somehow able to thrive as a couple without losing their identities. Their marriage had provided for him the joyful, grounded home, where he could recharge his batteries and plunge ahead, ready for any challenge his professional life threw at him.

After a few years, they were ready to share their joy with a child. Lucy was a tiny version of her mother, and displayed a mischievous, independent streak almost from birth. Luke could not fathom a world without Betsy and Lucy.

Chapter 6

March 1973 (Internship)

His beeper went off.

Doctor, your new patient is ready for you.

Nine months ago as a new intern, he'd first been called *Doctor*. He had a hard time getting used to it even now. He left the on-call room and strode down the polished floor of the corridor to the elevator, confident in his white coat, tie, and clean white pants. He was at ease.

Luke's confidence had grown over those grueling months. He felt the usual anxiety—what would it be this time?—but he was no longer panicky. Last summer, the adrenaline rush came from fright, foreboding, and a futile wish that he could be somewhere else. Sometimes he even wondered why he had chosen to be a doctor. Not only was he a doctor but also on any given night when his peers had gone home, he was *the* doctor. *He* was called and no one else. He couldn't flee. The nurse was calling him and only him. No escape, and always hoping his fear didn't show. That had been the worst of it: feeling that there was no way out.

Now his heart beat a little faster, but he was no longer scared. Eight months of constant pressure gave him more confidence than he ever would have imagined.

He watched the crowds of people pass by, laughing and talking on a sunny afternoon. He thought to himself, I own this corridor. At two a.m. when the halls are empty, I walk here, headed for the ER—clutching a cup of black coffee that tastes like liquid pencil lead, blood embedded under my nails, eyes burning with fatigue, stethoscope tucked away—off to slay another dragon. He wanted to tell passersby that it was his dominion. He felt a little bit crazy.

But he also thought of himself as a seasoned soldier. Like an infantryman who had survived winter at the Battle of the Bulge, he watched new recruits pour into battle, barely able to fire a rifle, panic written all over their faces. He was one of those baby-faced recruits last summer. Now he was a veteran, immune to death, brimming with cold confidence, even haughty—deservedly so, he thought.

What patients could he not handle? Arriving in cardiac arrest or diabetic coma, vomiting blood, in shock for unknown reasons, perhaps even cyanide poisoning. You name it, he had seen it. Or if not, he knew what to do when he did see it.

Start with the basics: Get an airway; make sure the heart is beating. Then deal with the cause. He remembered the old man on the medical ward a few months ago who had a cardiac arrest while on the commode late one afternoon.

Luke had been about to check out for a day off, his stomach growling. Just as he got to the elevator, he heard the intercom.

Code Blue, 923. Code Blue, 923.

He wheeled around and ran toward the commotion. He pushed his way in and saw an old man sitting on the commode, slumped over, his terrified wife trapped in the tiny bathroom next to him. She had pulled the emergency cord but could not get past him. Luke and the nurses dragged the gray, dying patient to the floor in the narrow space, then across the room, and heaved him onto the bed.

Luke's orders were calm. Using an Ambu bag from the emergency cart, a nurse forced air into his airways. Luke listened with his stethoscope over the man's chest and heard nothing. He leaned over and began chest compression. Cardiac leads were snapped into place and hooked to a monitor.

Get me a subclavian line. I need a number ten endotracheal tube. Shock him with four hundred joules. Everyone back away. Good—he's got a rhythm.

Luke had already ordered IV fluids, lidocaine, and dopamine to maintain his blood pressure.

OK, get him on a ventilator and transfer him to ICU.

He finished with a matter-of-fact laugh and a little hospital humor.

I could sure use a ginger ale.

Nothing could match that rush. He heard feigned ennui and nonchalance in his own voice.

Despite the worldly façade, he was only twenty-five years old and still thought of himself as a boy. Patients two and three times his age looked past his youth as they pleaded with him to make them better, or to keep them from dying.

Afterward, he stepped off the elevator and into another room, pulling back the curtain that surrounded the bed.

Hello, Mr. Fortier. I'm your doctor. He put out his hand.

What brings you to the hospital today?

You look so young, Doc.

Luke just smiled as he looked down at the handsome middle-aged man who could not hide his fear as he tried to keep the ill-fitting hospital gown from falling down his chest.

Luke knew well the nurse's drill: *Remove all your clothes and put on this gown, open to the back.* He could imagine this gentleman, a respected businessman, father and husband, losing his last shred of dignity as he climbed into the bed in a ward, his three roommates staring at the closed curtain, wondering about the new neighbor.

Luke pictured the man trying to climb beneath the covers with the gown riding up and his bare ass against the sheet. Luke pulled up a chair and sat in the crowded space with his clipboard, taking notes as he rattled off questions and listened for the answers.

Doc, I passed out at work. Someone called an ambulance and the next thing I knew, I was in the emergency room. They told me my blood count was low. I think they called it anemia. Said the low blood count made me dizzy. Apparently I fainted. They said I needed to come into the hospital for some tests.

He was pallid and looked scared.

I've never passed out before, Doc. What do you think is wrong?

Luke hedged.

We'll figure it out. It'll be OK, Mr. Fortier. First I need to ask you some questions and examine you. Then I will review the blood tests that they ordered in the ER.

Thanks, Doc. Whatever you say. You're in charge.

Hours later, night descended on the hospital. Visitors were gone; a skeleton crew of nurses moved quietly about under the subdued lights, taking temperatures, answering calls from patient rooms, meticulously measuring pills and doses into little paper cups in the medication room. The artificial light created an unreal form of daylight that could not mask the sad timelessness where patients lay alone to think about their illness, silently suffering from pain and depression, with no one to comfort them.

Televisions flickered behind the thin curtains that separated beds in the ward. The TV noise did a poor job of hiding the sounds of coughing, spitting, muttering, and the rustle of patients shifting positions in their beds.

Luke returned to the room, and stood outside the curtain.

Mr. Fortier?

He pulled back the curtain. His review of the blood work in the hematology lab had confirmed his worst suspicions. He sat in the chair beside the bed and looked his patient in the eye.

Mr. Fortier, you have a blood disorder called acute leukemia.

He gently explained that it was a cancer of the bone marrow where the uncontrolled white blood cell growth choked out the red blood cells, causing the anemia that led to the fainting spell.

Somehow, it was easier to say the words when he treated it like a tutorial delivered to a layperson. The textbook description, translated into plain English, took his mind off the gravity of the pronouncement. He knew it was a death sentence he was giving, couched in medical obfuscation. Anyway, now was not the time to drop the bomb.

The end of life lies somewhere down the road for everyone, sick or well. *You've got six months to live* is a common enough statement in fiction. The road for a terminally ill person can have a lot of twists and turns. Pain, suffering, hope, smiles, and tears all pave the way. What exactly is around each corner remains to be seen. But knowing the natural course of a terminal illness is like following a roadmap to a known destination. For those not facing such a disease, the road forward will be drawn over months and years. When and where it will end is a story yet to unfold. This was not the case for Mr. Fortier.

Is it serious, Doc?

The patient looked at him with subtle, but recognizable fright in his eyes. His voice was barely controlled. This man, father of three teenage children, a prominent civic leader and loyal husband, never before sick, was terrified. This man had fought in Korea, given himself selflessly to his family and community, asked little recognition for his achievements. He just wanted to know the truth so he could deal with it.

Yes, Mr. Fortier, it is serious. But we will make you better.

He only half believed what he had just uttered, but it was with a reassuring tone. He lied to give his patient a ray of hope because he knew how long the nights were for patients lying awake with nothing to think about, trying to sort out the fear, listening to their ward mates snore and moan, watching nurses move in and out like ghosts. This was no time to be brutally honest. Luke knew that soon enough, those long nights would come when his patient would lie alone in the dark, wondering about the lonely march down that hopeless road.

The patient exhaled a long sigh of relief.

OK, Doc. Thanks. Good night.

Luke sat at the nursing station and looked across the hall at the big clock. He summarized the clinical notes and wrote some orders. He thought about his patient and the painful treatment he would face over the next few months.

Acute myeloid leukemia. God, I hope we can cure it.

He knew it would be a long shot.

After a sunrise blood transfusion and a decent breakfast, Jean Fortier looked almost cheerful. *This man has courage*, Luke thought.

Mr. Fortier, we need to start chemotherapy right away.

Let's go. Just do what you have to do.

You need to know the side effects. This stuff is strong. I'm afraid it will make you sick to your stomach and give you diarrhea.

How else to say it?

You will lose your hair. But it will grow back.

We will start the chemotherapy here. Then you can go home. You will need to come back and forth to the hospital as we try to get this under control.

I can take it, Doc. Just make me better. I got a wife and kids who need me.

The days rolled by. Over the next few weeks of chemotherapy, Luke saw his patient vomiting into a plastic dish. He walked in one day as the nurses were turning him to one side so they could change the sheets he had just soiled with diarrhea. Luke was nauseated as he made rounds in the morning, and each day he saw a pile of cold scrambled eggs and soggy toast on the bedside tray, untouched.

He got to know Jean Fortier and knew in his heart that such intimacies would take its toll on him in the end. What could he do? Somehow he was drawn back to the bedside in the solitary night hours to talk to this man. Why, he couldn't say. But they fell into easy conversation that passed the time after visitors had gone, between calls, before it was time to sleep.

He learned a lot. Jean Fortier was the strong son of a French Canadian father. His family had emigrated from Quebec two generations ago to find a better life in America. His grandfather left a grueling life as a logger to work in the textile mills in Rhode Island. They were accustomed to hard work. He had grown up in Woonsocket, gone away to college, and returned to start a business and carry on a new generation, far away from the harsh life of his grandparents. He was prominent in his community, an honest, church-going man who gave a lot and asked very little.

Luke met Fortier's wife and children. He had become expert at cordiality. They could not see his despair and sadness when he saw them. But he knew they were slowly, but inexorably losing a husband and father.

The patient bore his suffering without complaint. When he finally left the hospital after three weeks, the timing of his return was unpredictable but inevitable. He did return only a few weeks later, then again and again, each time weaker, but never losing hope.

Luke was always there for him, even when Fortier was assigned to a different intern. Luke asked to be called when his patient returned. Though he was working in other wards and distracted by an endless stream of patients and exhausting nights, this special man was never far from his thoughts. Over time, he developed a relationship that was part doctor and part son. Paradoxically, he played the father to this man who could have been his father. It became clear, though unspoken, that death lurked closer as the days passed.

A point was reached when the chemotherapy was no longer effective. His bone marrow became engorged with leukemic cells. The red blood cells could easily be replaced by continued blood transfusions. But the loss of the white blood cells meant his immune system was shot. He acquired a bacterial bloodstream infection, sepsis.

Fortier lay in bed with chills so severe they caused his entire body to spasm. Heated blankets didn't help. Through it all he forced a smile when Luke came by to see him. But he would die unless they could somehow improve his immune system.

Luke met the hematology consultant at the nursing station and asked what else could be done. The hematologist told him there was a new technique being used where white blood cells from a donor could replace his defective immune system. The fix was temporary. It offered a reprieve until the bacterial infection that ravaged him could be suppressed. It required continuously withdrawing blood from one arm of the donor, running it through a set of filters to remove the white blood cells, then reinfusing the blood, absent the white blood cells, into the other arm.

The procedure took several hours and represented a total recirculation of the blood pool several times in order to produce a small bag of precious white blood cells that could be transfused into the patient to augment his failed immune system.

Where do you find donors?

As best we can tell, anyone with ABO blood group compatibility can donate the cells. But it's hard to get someone to go through the procedure because it's a new idea and takes several hours to collect the blood.

Luke didn't hesitate.

I'm O positive, so that makes me compatible. I want to help him.

The hematologist looked surprised.

OK. If you've got the time, come to my lab tomorrow afternoon and we'll do the procedure.

Luke arranged coverage of his patients by a fellow intern and showed up at the lab. He'd spent a long night wondering about the procedure, knowing that it was in the early stages of development. He'd never considered any dire possibilities—after months of frenzied coping with life-and-death emergencies, he felt himself immortal. To him this was just another way to do his best to help his patient. Luke lay on a stretcher and an assistant to the hematologist started an IV in his right arm with a needle that looked as big as a railroad spike. Then she repeated the same procedure in his left arm. The intravenous tubing was rigged up to a special machine that filtered out the white blood cells. They gave him a shot of heparin to thin his blood so clotting would not occur during the procedure.

He lay there, staring at the ceiling, with assistants huddled around and the machine whirring away. A few hours went by and his back and buttocks ached. He said nothing. He hoped the bag was filling with his healthy white blood cells. He thought of Jean Fortier lying in his hospital bed with a tormented, yet resigned look on his face. He told himself that a sore back was nothing when compared with the suffering of his dying patient.

Time passed. Finally, the hematologist returned.

OK, looks like we've got enough for a transfusion. Let's stop the procedure.

The machine went silent.

Then the assistant told him he needed a bolus of penicillamine to neutralize the heparin.

Otherwise you risk having a serious bleed.

They infused the drug into the intravenous line.

Suddenly, Luke couldn't breathe. His only thought was he was having a severe allergic reaction, anaphylaxis.

He felt like he was drowning, but somehow managed to croak a few words.

My lungs are filling up with fluid. Pulmonary edema.

He tried to push himself up.

I can't breathe! Help me!

The assistants called an emergency. He heard the familiar announcement over the intercom: *Code Blue, Hematology lab. Code Blue, Hematology lab.* The sounds were muffled by a roaring noise deep within his head, and he struggled to breathe. Somehow he thought about the absurd words, *Code Blue*, meaning there was a medical emergency that was broadcast throughout the hospital in such a way as to alert all the doctors but not throw all the patients and visitors into a panic.

What an irony. I am the emergency.

An anesthesiologist rushed into the lab in his green scrub suit. Luke was fading. Darkness began closing in.

He jolted awake. He vomited so hard he thought his intestines would evert.

Lying back, his chest heaving, he could breathe again.

The anesthesiologist anxiously watched over him for a few minutes.

Your body must have had a powerful reaction that reversed the allergic process and kept you from going into shock. It can happen sometimes — why, nobody knows. But if it had not, you likely would have had a cardiac arrest.

I'm still alive. I'm still alive.

Why it reversed itself he would wonder for years.

After recovering for a few hours, he refused to be hospitalized for overnight observation. Instead he walked back to his apartment on wobbly legs. That night his sleep was interrupted by the worst pounding headache he had ever experienced.

The next morning he watched the white blood

cells from the small plastic bag course down into his patient's vein. Luke felt bonded permanently to Jean Fortier.

The white blood cells seemed to help for a day or two. Fortier's fever came down.

It was a temporary reprieve. The fever returned with a vengeance and he began to slip in and out of consciousness, at times delirious.

Nothing was working to reverse the leukemia. A few nights later, Luke was called by a nurse.

Mr. Fortier wants to see you.

He ran up five flights of steps from his night duty in the ICU and stopped short of the door to catch his breath before entering.

It was late. Visitors were gone and the room was quiet except for the groans of Fortier's roommates. A dim light burned at the head of the bed, accentuating his ghostly appearance. Luke thought back to the pale, yet strong man he had first met a few short months ago.

Time stood still.

Doc, it's so good to see you. Thanks for coming. I'm dying, Doc. I know you did your best, but I'm dying. Hold my hand, Doc.

His voice was raspy, barely a whisper. His grasp was weak.

Luke held his hand. Grief permeated his entire body and froze him in place. The pain he felt was like a tattoo imprinted in his brain. The man's eyes closed, then opened, as though he were fighting to remain conscious.

He whispered, Doc, tell me, what do I say when I meet my Maker?

Luke wanted to respond, but had no answer. Whatever words he would have chosen got stuck in a suppressed sob. He shook his head and squeezed Fortier's hand. His eyes welled with tears. Jean Fortier closed his eyes for the last time.

Luke walked slowly into the dark on-call room and slumped down on the bed. Through the windows he could see the distant freeway where automobile lights ebbed and flowed endlessly. He wept.

Jean Fortier's last words played over and over in his head. How strange that a person grasped so firmly to a belief system that he needed to prepare for a conversation with God.

What kind of God would take a man like Jean Fortier, leaving a widow and three children to fend for themselves?

No atheists in foxholes. Why? Because when soldiers know death is staring them in the face, they need to grasp for the security they lost when they left the womb. Security they partly felt as young children with a teddy bear, or wrapped in their mother's arms.

Everything in life needed an explanation—even dying. The perpetual motion of the cars far below on the freeway, rounding the corner like a big, continuous circle, offered some solace. There was no end and no beginning. Everything was connected.

Luke wiped his eyes and walked back down to the ICU.

Chapter 7

April 1987 (Medical Practice — Year Ten)

Luke drove across town on an early April morning in a somber mood. He continued to be troubled. The dogwood trees all along University Drive had exploded into bloom, the predictable sequel to the azalea bloom that had followed the redbuds, as winter became spring. He knew that the late spring heat heralded another hot, long summer.

The warm morning brought back memories of the spring days at the beginning of his practice when he'd been energized at the thought of meeting each new day. Every moment, around every corner, there had been a spark of anticipatory excitement. He had felt ready for anything. Despite all the sickness and death, those days were sometimes spiced with levity, always a welcome if unpredictable reprieve.

He could not say when he began to feel differently about his life, but now, in the tenth year of his practice, the fun was gone. Something had happened to him that he could not identify—or shake off.

He parked his truck and walked to the first of three small houses in the cul-de-sac. Anyone who happened into the circular driveway off the quiet street would see three nicely maintained, single-story, ranch-style houses, typical concrete-block construction, nondescript. If a stranger had chanced to enter any of the three, he would have been shocked speechless.

After passing through a bare foyer, each house opened to a large room with a fake fireplace at one end. It was devoid of furniture. Four or five severely disabled adults lay on floor mats. Their diminutive forms were clothed and clean, but twisted into abnormal positions by severe contractures. A few were almost motionless. The others moved their arms and legs aimlessly. Three sat hunched over trays in high chairs fitted with wheels so their caregivers could move them around.

For many decades, severely disabled Floridians had been housed in several massive buildings across the state, all converted from tuberculosis hospitals. Families who could not or would not care for them could give them up to state-sponsored institutional care. The patients were mentally retarded, often profoundly so, and some had physical deformities and complex medical problems. The foreboding concrete buildings and their unfortunate inhabitants were collectively known as Palmland.

A valiant, if crude attempt was made to classify each patient according to the degree of mental and physical impairment. They were simply numbered, one through ten, according to increasing severity. Funding was limited, and their care was affected proportionally. The general public ignored them, frightening reminders of what could have been the case for anyone, but for a twist of fate.

A tour through one of these facilities would have shown cavernous rooms covered with padded mats where the most disabled patients lay, fed through nasogastric tubes with an unidentifiable gruel, and otherwise unattended. Those in wheelchairs were brought each morning to long porcelain sinks, formerly mortuary tables, for communal toothbrushing. Rats and cockroaches abounded. Large wall clocks ticked off the hours, month after month, year after year. A death would occur; a vacancy would be filled.

Then, several years ago a class-action suit was brought against the state by an advocacy group, comprised mostly of families touched by this unspeakable travesty. All Palmland institutions across the state were ordered to close within five years, releasing the inmates—*what else to call them?* Luke thought—into foster homes and other residential settings. The lawsuit convinced the court that these unfortunate ones had been warehoused and forgotten for far too long.

The legislative solution, in a collective fit of guilt, was to throw money at the problem in order to provide more personalized care in a community setting. The bureaucrats dutifully spent the available funds. Their interpretation of the mandate led to a newly coined word: mainstreaming. The first groups of Palmland residents to depart for the suburbs were the nines and tens, the most profoundly affected. Though of adult age, they appeared as physically mature children. They had immeasurably low IQs. All were afflicted with compounded medical conditions. They had to be cared for like defenseless infants.

Now that they were deinstitutionalized, the state referred to them as "clients."Luke had been asked to be the medical director of this group of twenty-four. They may have been "clients" to the state. To him, they were his patients.

The head nurse, Jane, greeted him warmly. He had often wondered how someone as young, bright and highly capable could have chosen to accept the position she held. Her job was to supervise the care and feeding of these poor souls, who were divided up among the three houses. Given their severity, she was responsible for managing a de facto intensive care unit with none of the technological support of a hospital.

Almost all these patients had troublesome seizure disorders. Some were fed through gastrostomy tubes that had been surgically placed directly through the abdomen into the stomach. Many had urinary catheters as well. Fever, respiratory infections, skin rashes and diarrhea were routine.

This small collection of houses was designated as a Cluster. It was a sanitized way to describe this bizarre living situation. *Clients in a Cluster. How alliterative.* In Luke's mind they were still forgotten people. Throwing tax dollars at the problem seemed to appease public guilt, a problem thrust into the lap of the legislature by the courts.

There was funding for twenty-four-hour nursing care. The law mandated physical and occupational therapy, which often amounted to blowing bubbles over a client's face and counting the times any measurable response, perhaps a smile, was seen. Surely they could be cared for in a less rigid, more loving way, than hidden on the end of a cul-de-sac, out of sight and mind.

Just as he did on other Tuesday mornings, Luke had arrived to make rounds. Jane walked with him. They stopped to see Jeff, once a thalidomide baby. He had stumps for hands, so-called phocomelia. He had blond, tousled hair and a toothy smile. His teeth were dotted with ugly amalgam fillings. Someone decided that cosmetic appearances did not matter when repairing dental caries for these people, so metal fillings were used back and front. Somehow, he also had been thought to be profoundly retarded. As a consequence, he had been institutionalized from birth, committed to a life with virtually no intellectual stimulation. Here at the Cluster, it became clear that he had cognitive ability, which had been masked by his inability to speak and his severe physical deformities. The staff began to take the time to look at him more closely. He responded to questions.

Jeff, do you like music? Jane asked. Jeff nodded enthusiastically and grinned. He had no speech except excited grunts.

She showed Luke how she had rigged up a chart on his tray table to allow him to add numbers and choose answers to questions. It was obvious that Jeff had been mistakenly classified years before as profoundly retarded, and left to live as a prisoner in his deformed body, unable to speak, deprived of education.

At the Cluster, he was fed with a spoon, sat in a chair, listened to music, watched the daily, monotonous activity around him, and was put to bed each night. He had no family, no visitors, no one except the nursing staff to care for him. He was thirty-five.

Jane had made a recent observation about Jeff. She prompted Luke to ask Jeff which Beethoven symphony was his favorite. When he did, Jeff shook his head excitedly, took his twisted forearm and pointed to the number five on the checkerboard of numbers on his table. Luke was speechless. It was a minor miracle that Jane could eke out enough time to make this discovery. He wondered how many of these individuals could have intelligence that no one had ever bothered to try to measure.

The two of them went from patient to patient, discussing their medical problems: seizure disorders, intractable constipation, pressure sores between the folds of their contracted arms and legs. They went to the other two houses and replayed their examination and discussion.

Luke saw one visitor, a silver-haired woman who quietly appeared several days a week to see her daughter, Mary. Jane told him that this elderly woman always sat with her daughter, caressed her contracted hands, and whispered to her in a soothing, tender voice. Her daughter gazed into space and occasionally shook as though she was startled. There was no apparent recognition. After an hour or two, her mother would pick up her handbag, thank the nurses for their gentle care, and walk sadly out the door. No one else ever entered the buildings aside from the health-care staff.

He drove away. The isolation and societal abandonment of these twenty-four human beings weighed on him. Even when he had to transfer one of them to the hospital, specialists he consulted treated them impersonally: add an anticonvulsant, adjust an antibiotic, insert a gastrostomy tube, replace a urinary catheter. There was no discussion of them as patients, just a perfunctory note in the hospital chart. A service was provided for a fee.

Not infrequently, the entire group was trundled into vans for fieldtrips. Wheelchairs were raised up on lifts and fixed to the van floor. Arms and legs flailed; catheters were attached. Bibs covered their chests to manage the uncontrollable drooling; diapers and other gear were bundled into bags. The entire affair took up the better part of a day. They would reach a park where the whole process needed to be undone. Eventually, with his patients strapped firmly into position, all their wheelchairs were lined up in a row, to face a band concert off in the distance.

They were all but invisible to passersby. Only their caregivers paid them any attention. To be sure, preachers would say they were children of God. It was as though such a proclamation satisfied any further need to attend to them as human beings. They were, forever, someone else's problem.

Any thought of these societal castoffs only arose to the level of acknowledgment by ordinary people was when it was proposed a Cluster be installed in a given neighborhood. Then a groundswell of complaints ensued, demanding they not be allowed to domicile in the neighborhood. Not in my backyard, they would say.

Chapter 8

March 1987 (Medical Practice — Year Ten)

The redbuds were long gone, replaced by azaleas in profusion all over town. But for some reason, the season this year did not hold the promise of past springs.

Luke was finally done with one more meaningless hospital committee meeting that had stolen an hour from his day. It was early afternoon. He passed the window on the seventh floor where the sun beat in. He looked down to the loading zone. A dumpster off in the far corner stood askew, dropped unceremoniously from a refuse truck. No need to place it carefully since it was the sole occupant of a big, hot concrete space.

Luke stopped and walked back to the window and stared down. Every corner of the hospital conjured up a memory. He vividly recalled a coed who had come to his office one afternoon two years before when the azaleas were in bloom. She was a striking, petite blonde; not surprisingly, a sorority girl. She reminded him of a frail bird, quivering ever so slightly.

Her voice shook as she related her story. She'd contracted genital herpes from a casual sexual partner and sought the advice of an infectious disease specialist. He had explained to her that once a person was infected, the virus took up residence in a nerve nucleus where it lay dormant. Then, for unknown reasons, the virus would travel down the neuron to the skin, and produce painful, itchy blisters. Over a few weeks, the lesions would heal, as the virus returned to its home in the cell nucleus. He had added, however, that the blisters on her labia would recur at unpredictable intervals.

As she continued her story, she clasped her hands in her lap, then paused before she told Luke how it hurt to bear the thought that she was permanently infected—and contagious to any future sexual partner. He sensed that it had become her own scarlet letter, an obsession from which she could not escape. She was apparently tormented day and night, knowing she could not free herself from this sexual chain letter.

She had come to Luke for a second opinion. She leaned forward and asked what he thought. He recalled trying to reassure her.

He spoke gently. Yes, as best we can tell, the infection is permanent. But there are a few things you need to know. First, it is the same virus that causes cold sores—who hasn't had one on their lip at one time or another? In that case the virus lives in a nerve that supplies the skin around the mouth. Second, you know the infection called chicken pox? It is caused by a virus called Varicella and causes skin blisters, which then heal. That virus also lives in the neuron. Later in life it can reappear as a disease called shingles. Why does it come back? No one knows. These viruses are widely accepted as a fact of nature.

Her face was expressionless. She nodded at his words. Luke had assumed she understood. He advised her to see a counselor to talk through her concerns. She stood, offered a wan smile, said thank you, and left.

Two weeks later she walked through the door of the hospital, took the elevator to the seventh floor, and stood by this very window. He pictured her there, withdrawn into herself, oblivious to her surroundings. Then she was gone.

He looked down to the concrete. The blood had long since washed away. He wondered about her thoughts as she stood before this window. She would have had to scrunch herself down to get through the small space. At what point did gravity pull her out? He wondered what she thought as she slipped away through space, out this very window, with the same hot sun beating through it.

Thousands of people had walked down this hallway since the moment when this window had become the escape hatch from a tortured life. How many of them remembered anything about her? He remembered. He saw the ghost.

How might he have done better? Could he have read her emotions better? Could he have stopped her from ending her life? For him, the memory would never leave. For her, there would be no more memories.

Luke took the elevator down and walked back across the street to his office. The relentless midday heat and humidity distracted him from thoughts of the girl. The cool office was a relief from a long morning of constant hospital demands.

He took a chart from the pocket outside an exam room and walked in. There sat Essie Williams. He felt a sudden surge of relief from his increasingly negative state of mind. Essie had that effect on him. For all the difficulties life threw at her, she always remained pleasant.

He smiled at her, recalling the first day he'd seen her.

Hello Miz Williams, what can I do for you?

Doc, my name is Essie. You can call me Essie. Don' want no "Miz Williams."

Today she looked dignified as she sat straight-backed in the chair, like she had been there and could stay there forever, statue-like.

Essie looked straight at him with her deep penetrating black eyes, round onyx gems that sparkled in the reflected light and were set off by prominent, sculpted cheekbones. Though sixty years old, her handsomeness belied her age.

Her features and posture gave her a proud look. Her heritage might be from the Gullah culture, a black population that had colonized the barrier islands along the southeast coastline. It was a forced ancestry from Angola and other West African countries. The Gullah people had retained their racial homogeneity despite the ravages of slavery, and had stayed in the area after the Civil War. From the way Essie carried herself, she could have descended from royalty. Her visage brought to his mind the famous tintype photograph of Sitting Bull that immortalized—perhaps mythologized—the man. It was a haunting image that represented an entire race, wiped off the planet, justified and dismissed through several centuries of untold suffering, forgotten or at least erased from US history books.

To him, Essie was a black female Sitting Bull. Like everyone, she likely had her flaws, but her striking appearance hid whatever failings she may have had. Her big hands, calloused from decades of field work, clutched the black, plastic purse that held the spit jar for her snuff, and could have held half her belongings, given its size.

The spanking-clean cotton dress she wore had been subjected to countless hand washings over many years. It was simple but elegant. She wore a black wig, curly, and just short enough to lend an

air of self-satisfied sophistication. He never understood why it always sat just slightly crooked. He
was sure she looked at her reflection in a mirror to
satisfy herself that she was just so—*Goin' to the
doctor.* She wore no stockings and her feet were
adorned with high-top black Converse All Star
sneakers, the kind that had been popular thirty
years ago, now relegated to the Kmart shoe
department.

There she sat, vintage Essie. Her poise masked
her difficult life. Essie had grown up in a two-room
shotgun shack, surrounded on four sides by
furrows that stopped right at the walls in order to
maximize space for planting. Her family had been
sharecroppers. She'd slept in the only bed with her
siblings and her parents. The planks on the raised
floor had cracks so big the ground was visible
below. The other room had a few ragged chairs and
a potbellied stove. Essie still wore the scars on her
legs from being burned by the hot stove as a small
girl.

She had almost no formal schooling. She had
spent her childhood toiling in the fields, helping
her family subsist with almost no possessions and
barely enough food. Her parents had died long ago
and her brothers and sisters were scattered, trying
to eke out a living however they could.

Essie's whole world consisted of the rundown
double-wide she lived in with her husband. Many
years before, she had given birth at home with only

a midwife to help her through a prolonged, painful labor. Her baby had been born dead with the umbilical cord wrapped around her neck. She knew it was a girl, and they had buried her next to the trailer.

Essie had continued to bleed after the delivery and was brought to the small hospital in Cedar Grove. The general practitioner told her he had to perform a hysterectomy, which he did. She knew there would be no more pregnancies. She mourned the loss of her baby girl, then soldiered on.

Since that time she and Wilbur had worked in the fields, always struggling to keep food on the table. Luke knew vaguely where they lived, down a dirt road outside the crossroads village called LaCrosse. It could have been any dirt road outside LaCrosse, Milton, Galesburg, Cedar Grove—all towns that surrounded Tallahassee. Populated mostly by poor blacks, nothing had changed there for well over a hundred years.

Mostly on a Sunday afternoon, the men, Wilbur among them, could be seen congregating around a picnic table, typically sheltered beneath an ancient canopy of live oaks, from which Spanish moss hung languidly beneath the baking sun. They laughed and joked and drank whiskey from paper bags, smoking and spitting, happy to be among friends. Wilbur, as Essie, lacked any formal education. Nevertheless, he could operate any kind of heavy equipment better than anyone: forklifts, tractors, backhoes, graders. He was proud of his skills, but never bragged. Mostly he was thankful to have a full-time job, whereas most of his friends were relegated to the backbreaking work of a sharecropper or part-time caretaker.

The two of them had nothing but a powerful spirit and a kindness that Luke had never encountered before. Once, when they were very low on cash, Wilbur came for an office visit. Looking embarrassed, he'd said, Doc, I recollected you knowed about fatwood, so I brought you a stump in trade if it sits wi' you.

They walked out to the parking lot.

Fatwood, or lighter stump as they sometimes called it, was a name given to centuries-old pine stumps. The resin concentrated in it such that a few sticks were enough to kindle a fire. The bed of Wilbur's pickup had enough kindling to last for ten years. Wilbur insisted he take the whole thing.

Today, something in Essie's face betrayed a sadness, despite her perpetual smile. Her predictable friendliness was disarming.

Hey, Doc. Ha' you?

I'm doin' OK, Essie. Nice to see you.

He wasn't OK, but how he felt was not why Essie was there. Part of him wanted to tell her he was tired. Medical practice was wearing him down. There was no longer a moment when he was not on a phone call about another emergency. The weight he carried like an invisible millstone never lightened. Thoughts coursed through his brain like a ticker tape, day and night. Had he missed a diagnosis? Would a patient have a life-threatening reaction to a drug he prescribed? He could think of hundreds of random reasons why his phone might ring. It was never good news.

He snapped out of his distracted, self-pitying reverie.

Essie gripped a small piece of gauze between two fingertips where a finger-stick puncture had been done by his nurse to coax a drop of blood for a glucose test.

How you feeling, Essie? I see your sugar level is way up. It's four hundred. You been taking your diabetes medicine?

Shonuf, Doc. Been takin' 'em right smart. But Doc, I ain't gonna lie. I be runnin' low dem sugar pills, and I ain't got no money these days. Times been real hard. So I cuts 'em up to make 'em last, but I run slap out a few days back. Ain't had no work pickin' past few months, so we run kinda low. But I gotcha sump'in here.

She lifted a large grocery bag from the floor next to her and handed it to him.

You tol' me you like dem biled peanuts, so here's a mess of em'. Picked 'em when they was green yes'day, biled em up wi' salt. They be mighty good.

Essie's cheeks darkened ever so slightly. He took her hand in his and met her eyes. They were stoic, but she was unable to hide her fear.

Sorry you ran out of pills, Essie. Let's get you some samples to tide you over. I've got a bunch. I'll get you enough so you don't need to worry.

He bolted from the room.

What kind of a society do we live in where hardworking people like Essie and Wilbur have to scrape and beg just to stay alive? They ask for so little—and are given less.

He opened the medicine closet and grabbed the sample boxes of Micronase, packed neatly with eight to a box. There was more packaging than medicine. He emptied the boxes and left them on the shelf. His anger welled up.

Tammie! Call the drug rep and get as many of these blasted Micronase samples as they can spare. Now!

Luke realized he was shouting and took a deep breath before taking the handful of pills back to Essie.

Doc, it ain't me I worries about.

She opened her purse, unscrewed the lid of the small jar inside, and discreetly spit tobacco juice into it.

Doc, Wilbur los' his job and we gots no mo' medical 'surance. An' we ain't got 'nuf money to pay you wi'.

Essie, what happened?

When Luke had seen Wilbur six months ago, he'd complained of peeing blood. A number of tests showed he had polycystic kidney disease, a

genetic condition where cysts formed on the liver
and kidneys. Luke told Wilbur it was nothing he
could have prevented. He'd been born with it, and
it did not show itself until he was middle-aged. The
kidney cysts were filled with blood, and likely the
trauma from the road equipment caused a cyst to
rupture, sending blood through the urinary tract.
Worse, his kidneys had begun to fail because of the
disease.

He had referred Wilbur to a nephrologist. The
specialist told Wilbur he'd need dialysis sometime
in the near future. Until then, there was nothing
more he could do, and he sent Wilbur back to Luke.

By then his kidney function had gotten worse.
Luke reassured Wilbur that he would help him as
much as he could. Now this.

Essie continued. Well, Doc, Wilbur come home
one day a few weeks back. Said the boss man tol'
him those medical bills be too high. Said he could
not pay the 'surance premiums for the other
workers. Said he could only 'ford the 'surance if
Wilbur was off the payroll. Said he was sorry.
Hoped Wilbur could find other work.

Essie's eyes welled up. Luke felt rage and pity;
he kept his voice gentle.

Essie, I'll do whatever I can to make sure
Wilbur gets the care he needs.

His words rang hollow in his own ears. He
knew he could not get kidney dialysis when Wilbur
needed it. Dialysis centers were not in the business

to provide a service to patients with no money. They would trot out the predictable mantra that they could not afford to dialyze patients without reimbursement. Government insurance would eventually pay for it, but not during the several month waiting period before coverage began. Until then there was no insurance coverage. Wilbur would be expected to pay out of his own pocket. Luke knew he would have to beg specialists to see Wilbur for no payment, and he would somehow have to finagle lab and X-ray tests.

Essie collected the drug samples and dropped them into her big pocketbook. Then she took out a small handkerchief and dabbed her eyes. She offered one more stoic smile, then rose and walked slowly out the door, standing tall with her head bowed. She knew that Wilbur would not live much longer.

Chapter 9

May 1987 (Medical Practice — Year Ten)

Spring lasts a long time in north Florida, but never long enough. People savor the days, knowing that summer is just around the corner. As soon as the dogwood blossoms disappear, the searing heat takes over. The long summer days drag into months, during which the enervating combination of heat and humidity drives people into the air-conditioned indoors at least from dawn to dusk if at all possible.

This year, the oppression of summer seemed to Luke to come earlier and weigh heavier on body and spirit. One day during this foreboding time, an insurance salesman came to Luke's office with a litany of complaints. His symptoms were vague. His monotonic presentation sapped the doctor's rapidly waning energy. The salesman sat in the chair in his short-sleeved white shirt and loosened tie, droning on and on about various aches, pains, headaches, fatigue, insomnia, and other miscellaneous gripes.

Surely, the man surmised, I must have a serious disease. It has to be something bad, like cancer—maybe something rare and serious.

Somehow, the idea that his symptoms could be stress-related was humiliating. Ironically, he, like many others, would rather have a more socially acceptable diagnosis than depression. *I have cancer*, he could say at the next cocktail party when asked why he looked so wan. That would be much more comfortable than saying, *All my symptoms are apparently due to depression*. He would much prefer to admit to, perhaps, chronic fatigue syndrome, Lyme disease, or fibromyalgia—anything but anxiety or depression.

In the course of their conversation, Luke uncovered the reason for the man's complaints.

Doc, my life is so boring. I get up every day, drive to work and sell insurance. That's all I do. You are a doctor. You must have an exciting life, seeing all kinds of interesting problems, dealing with life and death.

He made it sound like a movie script.

Maybe there was a time when Luke had felt like he was starring in his own movie. That time had long since passed. He recalled the admonition of his mentor so many years before. . His internship had become the best year of his life. It had to be, or it would have been the worst. He remembered a

fellow intern, David, who was always miserable.
Every word that came out of his mouth was
negative. The work hours were too long; he was
always exhausted; patients were an intrusion; the
nurses were incompetent.

His attitude permeated his entire being, and he
paid for it day after day. The nurses exacted their
revenge. In the deepest hours of the night when, as
happened all too frequently, a sleeping patient's IV
got caught in the sheets and fell out, it was the
intern's job to get out of bed and restart it. But the
night nurses knew how exhausted the interns were
and graciously restarted the IV themselves to let
the intern sleep. That is, unless the intern had
gotten on their bad side.

David would get a call.

Doctor, I can't seem to get the IV started, you'd
better do it.

For him the night nurse never seemed able to
restart an IV. It was sweet revenge.

One night David lay exhausted in the on-call
room. The phone rang. A patient with gastroin-
testinal bleeding had suddenly begun passing fresh
clots of blood from his rectum. He was bleeding
profusely—a medical emergency. He mumbled to
the nurse to increase the flow of the IV fluids and
fell back to sleep. At the risk of incurring his wrath,
she called again as the patient's blood pressure
began to fall. He said he'd be right there, then just
rolled over. The third time, a nurse banged on his

door. By then the patient was in shock from blood loss. They were unable to revive him. David claimed no recollection of the first two calls. The intern had lost his edge.

He didn't see David again, but assumed that they had not crossed paths because of mind-numbing workloads on different clinical rotations. Several months later he learned that David had dropped out of the internship program.

Yes, that year had to have been the best of Luke's life. And it *was* like a movie. He had to be hypervigilant at all times, ready to jump from bed like a fireman when called. A negative mindset would have been disastrous. The total exhaustion of the internship was only manageable with a posi-tive, aggressive frame of mind. His colleague had proved the point.

That was a long time ago.

The salesman was still talking.

Doc, if only I could have your life.

The fire Luke carried from those bygone years was burning low. He no longer had that heady confidence to energize him. The walls were closing in. Practicing medicine was wearing him down. He was like a tire with too many miles; the tread was nearly gone.

Maybe I need a vacation.

The problem was that when he left his office for a week, he paid triple. First there was the cost of the vacation for him and his family. Second, he bore the cost of keeping his office open and his staff employed to answer the phones, refill prescriptions, perform billing functions, and refer patients who needed immediate attention to other doctors. Third, the income he would have generated during the week was lost.

He continued to worry constantly about hundreds of patients he had treated within recent memory, not to mention the thousands that he had cared for many months or years before. Where were they? How were they doing? Why had he not seen them in so long? Did they move, die, change doctors? It was rare for a patient to return to say thank-you. He accepted that. It was like a drowning swimmer who is saved by the lifeguards and then, more often than not, scuttles away without so much as a thank-you. He supposed that what seemed like ingratitude was likely due to embarrassment, or the need to put a close call with death behind them.

He hoped they recovered, were well, felt gratitude if he had made them better.

His patients may have been left with a sense of relief; he was left with a void. One he remembered vividly was Carrie McCarthy, a beautiful dark-haired woman with meningitis. She was carried into his office in a coma after her fiancé had found her unconscious in her apartment. The man was terrified. Luke had seen enough meningitis to know that she would live. He could even assure the distraught man that within three days—after a spinal tap, penicillin, and vital systems support— she would awaken from her coma, as if awakening from sleep. And she did.

They married, and Carrie sent Luke a dozen white roses on his birthday for several years afterward as thanks. Such gestures were rare. Finally, the couple realized that it was OK to move on. The roses stopped coming.

Mostly, Luke lived with the memories of incomplete stories, wondering whether he had fulfilled his obligation as a physician, not knowing about the ultimate outcomes of so many people. They were ghosts lurking in the back of his mind. Any time his pager buzzed or the phone rang from the emergency room, it felt like a cattle prod, and his first thought was that one of those countless patients had come back. The best year—his internship—had passed.

Chapter 10

May 1987 (Medical Practice — Year Ten)

Death is a simple word that has echoed through the entire history of humankind. It has been discussed, written about, and feared. To Luke, no matter how it was studied, parsed, or avoided, it always came back to finality. When a life ended and Luke pronounced a patient dead, all the emotional baggage he had carried like a millstone around his neck disappeared. All the details were erased in an instant. There were no more questions about the hemoglobin level, the IV fluids to order, the potassium level, and a thousand dials to twist trying to keep the patient alive, or at least allowing the demise to happen without causing it.

Patients died in so many different ways. Sometimes an elderly stroke victim simply stopped breathing. That was the easiest. He conjured up a mental image of one old man who'd died early in the morning. His wife of many years sat next to his bed, gently moving her hand over his thin white hair, quietly crying. The old man was waxy-pale and still. A man he remembered as feisty and affable now looked like a store mannequin. His feelings toward the old guy seemed to die with the physical death. He did feel bad for the diminutive, loyal widow, so fragile and lost. What had become of her, he did not know. When he closed the hospital chart and completed the death certificate, it was over. On to the next battle.

The act of dying, from whatever cause, is so quick; it is truly like a candle being extinguished. A life that had burned brightly suddenly goes dark. Nothing remains but a curl of smoke.

He was continually amazed at how the final moment could occur so fast, without fanfare. Hollywood images have ingrained in the public mind that the act of dying lasts for minutes, if not hours, with each second a separate videographic frame. In fact, nothing is further from the truth. Once the heart stops, so does the brain. It happens in seconds.

To him, death itself was not troubling. No, it was the process of dying that was so gut-wrenching and fraught with emotional tension as to be almost intolerable. He thought back to his internship, to a memory that remained as vivid now as it was nearly two decades ago.

Four teenagers had been brought to the emergency room after a head-on car collision. They were all attired in formal wear, having attended their senior prom. Each was rolled in on a stretcher. All four were dead from head injuries. He recalled the shock of seeing them. Though there was dried and matted blood on their heads and nostrils, their suits and formal gowns were intact. In the glare of the overhead lights, they looked like adult-size dolls. He never knew them in life. He wondered what their last thoughts were—alive, then dead.

In the same train of thought, he recalled a patient rushed into the emergency room, sitting on the stretcher, vomiting into a basin. He had been in a drunken quarrel with his wife. As an employee at a jewelry factory, he had access to cyanide. He laced his beer with it— to prove to his wife how desperate he was to end his miserable life — and drank it down. Within ten minutes the emergency medical technicians had rushed him through the swinging doors of the ER. Between episodes of retching, the patient confessed what he had done.

Luke remembered his almost casual instruction to the nurse.

Get the cyanide antidote pack.

He knew the formula: an infusion of 3 percent sodium nitrite followed by 25 percent sodium thiosulfate. He also knew the man would likely die in front of his eyes before they could give him the antidote. And that was exactly what happened. The cyanide in his blood froze the hemoglobin, so no oxygen could be released to his brain or anywhere else.

The man, alive, was suddenly dead. His skin was still warm and pink. Luke was still in the grip of the frightening excitement of trying to prevent death, to halt the process of dying. But it was too late. The act of dying was over before the antidote could turn it around. Life had become death.

The dead man was covered with a sheet and wheeled to the back hall, awaiting the trip to the morgue. His color remained so lifelike, as cyanide poisoning leaves it, that Luke, as a young doctor, had walked back and lifted the sheet to convince himself that the man was dead.

Now, Luke obsessed about the hundreds of his patients who had died. What continued to haunt him was their dying, not their deaths. All the efforts to stop the inexorable slide from life to no-life; the pain; the terror in the patient's eyes, begging to be saved; the shattered emotions of families and friends; the pressure to do something to stop the runaway train—these experiences were what wrung him out, not death itself.

Each one seemed to chip away a bit of his own life. Was it his imagination, or had he been increasingly assaulted of late with dying patients? Did he expect anything different? After all, he had chosen to be a pulmonologist. It had once been a thrill to look down the airways with a flexible bronchoscope, to capture a piece of tissue between two tiny stainless steel jaws, then to withdraw the tube and put the fragment in a small vial to be analyzed by a

rocedure was like a challenging
.nen it was done, he had felt a self-
.u rush.

When the diagnosis of lung cancer came back,
he would switch into a routine treatment mode—
chemotherapy, radiation, perhaps surgery. In the
early days, he'd thought the patient would be a
clinical challenge to be faced, more than a human
being with a past, a job, a family.

Studying the lungs was both enjoyable and
challenging. It had all the right mix—interesting
physiology, the endoscopic game, a lot of time
spent adjusting ventilator settings in the ICU. They
called him in emergencies because he knew all the
tricks and had the skill and knowledge to use them.
Pulmonary disease was a natural for him. Of
course dying and death were part of it. Who would
not expect someone with a lifelong history of
smoking to die of lung cancer or some other lung
disease? Smokers destroyed their lungs over
decades and consequently, spent their last years
starved for oxygen—finally to die, if not from
cancer, then from emphysema or another chronic
obstructive pulmonary disease. Their lives would
be reduced to that cruel acronym, COPD.

It was hard to get close to these patients,
unfortunate as they were. For decades, despite
repeated warnings, they had chosen to ignore the
damage to their lungs caused by cigarettes. Their
many years of inhaling smoke had simply taken

its toll. Nonetheless, it was painful to see them beg to be able to breathe. He tried to help them, adjusting their medicines and reassuring them. But in a way, he saw their demise as the result of a Faustian bargain. They could not turn back the clock.

He did not relish the last days, even months, when these weary souls looked up at him with pleading eyes as they pursed their lips and gasped for breath. There may be no worse death than being starved for oxygen, day and night. They lost weight, as every ounce of energy was spent just trying to get oxygen into their lungs, even as their brains screamed for more and more. He had learned to accept the situation. He tried to treat each one as an individual, rather than just another lung-disease patient, and always sought some way to adjust their medications to ease the unstoppable downhill spiral. When death came, he knew they could finally rest, and so could he—until the next such patient.

He could not have foreseen the events that unfolded years earlier, throwing a curveball at him. The Centers for Disease Control published a brief report on four gay men in Los Angeles who developed a lung infection stemming from an odd germ called Pneumocystis. It was a fungus rather than a bacteria or virus. Personally, he had seen only a few cases in his entire career.

He knew this rare microbe could cause the lungs to fill with fluid and inevitably lead to death within a few weeks or even days. Despite the use of ventilators, treatment with a powerful drug called pentamidine, intensive support of falling blood pressure and the failure of other body functions, he was not surprised that the infected men died.

Strangely, Pneumocystis lived in the environment in symbiotic harmony with all the other fauna and flora that grew side by side in the Petri dish known as planet Earth. The only time Pneumocystis turned killer was in individuals who had lost their natural immune defenses. Mostly, it was found in cancer patients treated with chemotherapy which knocked out their immune system as a side effect. They became susceptible to infection with this germ, and it took advantage of their reduced defenses.

Pneumocystis virtually never infected a person with normal immunity. Why these young men had acquired this infection was at first a frightening mystery.

A lot had been learned since then. The reason they developed this strange infection was that their immune systems had been destroyed. But if they had not received chemotherapy, what had destroyed their immune system? The culprit was a virus that was not identified until two years later: human immunodeficiency virus, or HIV. There was no history of it infecting humans until it first emerged in Africa a few decades earlier. A similar virus was found in lower primates, and scientists speculated that the virus had mutated and begun to infect humans who had been exposed to primate blood. One thing appeared clear: the virus somehow entered a human's bloodstream and destroyed the white blood cells that circulate as an immune surveillance mechanism.

During those first few years, HIV was almost always found in homosexual men and popularly called a gay disease, likely transmitted by repeated, traumatic sexual activity. It spread like wildfire across the United States because no one knew they had acquired the infection until their immune system was shot. At that point, they were labeled with the diagnosis of acquired immunodeficiency syndrome, or AIDS.

After AIDS was diagnosed, the victim was at risk of being overtaken by any number of bizarre illnesses, such as Pneumocystis pneumonia. They could be afflicted with grotesque purple blotches on their skin that also developed internally—a cancer called Kaposi's sarcoma. They could contract tuberculosis or cryptococcosis or cytomegalovirus infection. They became susceptible to common infections like staphylococcus. Once they had AIDS, the available treatment was almost completely ineffective. It was a death sentence that could take them within weeks, months, or at most, a few years.

It did not take long to realize that HIV could be transmitted by exposure to contaminated blood from a number of sources. In the early days of HIV, it was impossible to detect the virus in the blood-stream. Thus, infected blood from donors was transfused to patients who needed blood. People with hemophilia had many transfusions over years and HIV infection became epidemic. Drug users who shared dirty needles began infecting one another.

Over the past three years, like everyone else, Luke had watched the horror of a virus that caused near panic in the population. Speculation was rampant. A rumor was spread that the virus could be transmitted by mosquito bites. Unproven allegations arose, maintaining that casual exposure to an infected person could cause the virus to spread. No one appeared safe from this modern scourge of biblical proportions.

Each time a rumor was disproved, doubters rose up from all corners of society, such as fundamentalist preachers who claimed the virus was a punishment from God, or charlatans who contended that they could cure it with holistic healing methods. Virtually all who doubted that medical science was being truthful spouted their own theories. As a consequence, even physicians who were grounded in science became afraid.

Many of the diseases afflicting AIDS patients involved the lungs. Luke had chosen a challenging, mainstream medical specialty in which he could ride the ebb and flow, was assaulted suddenly with an entirely new group of patients. He saw himself being labeled the AIDS doctor.

It was insidious at first. A patient would appear in his office, referred by a colleague who had recommended him because of his expertise in lung infections. Fair enough. But soon thereafter, patients diagnosed with HIV infection—even before they developed AIDS—began to show up, referred for no particular reason except the implied notion that they might get a lung infection if and when they developed the disease.

One patient with AIDS had been sent to Luke's office by a thoracic surgeon. The patient had a severe chest infection that started in the lung and was working its way through the chest wall. Called *Empyema necessitans,* the infection was a pus pocket so extensive that it pushed its way from the lungs, through the rib cage and eventually broke through the skin of the chest. Until the advent of AIDS, this condition had rarely been seen since antibiotics were introduced four decades previously.

The patient had been referred to the thoracic surgeon by a general practitioner because the massive infection needed to be drained with a large tube bored through the skin into the abscess cavity. Draining the blood and pus into a collection bottle relieved the pressure and was the only way to cure the infection. The drainage procedure was routine for a doctor trained in thoracic surgery.

Luke was confused when the patient showed

up in his office. The man, short of breath from the pain, had managed a few words.

The surgeon told me you would be the best doctor to take care of me.

The explanation made no sense, so he called the surgeon to clarify the patient's remark.

This guy has AIDS. I have a wife and two children and I am concerned that I could become infected with the virus in the case of blood contamination.

I have a young child, too, Luke replied. How is my personal situation any different?

Well, I don't know what to tell you, but I won't do the procedure.

Luke hung up the phone and went back to the patient whose chest wall was bulging out as he labored to breathe. Luke drained the abscess. The need to concentrate on a procedure in which he was not highly skilled drove away his anger at the surgeon.

Not long afterward he saw an elderly couple in his office. They had retired and were traveling in their Airstream mobile home. It was not unusual for snowbirds to pass through town on their way north or south, so their presence did not surprise him. When he opened the door to the exam room, the husband got up. He was tall, gray haired, and somewhat bent over. He offered a weak handshake and thanked the doctor for seeing them. His wife sat quietly in the corner chair. They appeared both frightened and shy. The three of them were cramped in a room that also held an exam table.

He went through the usual introduction and began asking them questions. The husband said they were from Ohio and sketched the plan they had undertaken to travel around the country after his retirement two years before. They had sold their home and met with other members of the vagabond group known as the Good Sam Club. They planned to meet their new friends at various campgrounds and had been excited to hit the road in their small RV.

So, you retired at age sixty-seven and you've been on the road since then?

Yeah, we thought it would be the right time, especially after my wife had suffered bleeding in her intestines from a diverticulum a couple of years before. She almost died. They gave her eight units of blood.

He nodded at his wife. She just sat, stoic, barely looking up.

It sounds like you had a good plan.

The man looked directly at Luke. His voice took on a somewhat angry tone, but it was controlled.

Well, Doc, it didn't work out so good. A year after we got going, she started up with fevers. He nodded toward his wife. She stared silently at her hands clasped in her lap.

I took her to the doctor back in Akron. He did

all kind of tests and said her white blood cells were low. Then he did an HIV test on her and it came back positive. I said, HIV? What's that? He said, It's the virus that causes AIDS. She's got AIDS.

His wife kept very still, and continued to look down.

The man told Luke that the doctor in Akron felt sure she had gotten the virus from a contaminated blood transfusion back before they could test it to see whether it was infected. When she got the fevers again, he did some more tests and they showed real low white blood cells, so he started treating her with AZT.

Doc, we know she's got AIDS. His face was impassive.

And when they tested me, they found out I was carrying the virus, too. So, the reason we're here is because she needs her AZT. We don't go back to Ohio anymore, and we need a doctor who knows us so we can get her medicine.

Of course I'll help you. But how often do you come through here? And do you have friends and family that can help?

We stay at campgrounds. None of our friends know anything about AIDS. They think it's a gay disease, and there must be something wrong with a person who gets it. So, we don't tell nobody. We got two kids with families, and we haven't told them either, cuz we're afraid they won't under-stand and won't want to see us for fear of somehow getting the virus.

His wife looked pallid. She hadn't said a word. Luke looked at the face of a man who had aged ten years in a few short months. He looked straight ahead, expressionless.

Luke knew what they were in for. He saw the pain and loneliness crushing them, as the harsh fluorescent light of the exam room glared down from the ceiling. The man lowered his head and his shoulders slumped, as if the ensuing days and weeks were more than he could bear.

Luke tried to reassure them and encouraged them to share their burden with someone who could provide support. The woman would become very ill in the near future and would die. He envisioned them alone, stranded in some unknown place. He was well aware that his words sounded hollow in that small room.

He wrote a prescription and said an uncomfortable good-bye. Their handshakes were limp with futility and mental exhaustion. They thanked him and he watched them leave the office—a pathetic scene, the old man holding the door for his wife. He pictured them, night after night, staring at the specter of her imminent death, seated over a simple dinner in their motor home at some godforsaken trailer park. Time would march them down a slow, narrow road to the inevitable.

They never came back.

When Luke let his mind wander, now more

than ever, it seemed, he was deluged with a flood of memories. It seemed as though everyone had or would have AIDS. They were all linked, like a chain.

His next AIDS patient was a convict with pneumonia who had been transferred to his hospital from the state penitentiary, thirty miles away. The prison hospital was manned uniformly by marginally trained foreign medical school graduates. Any prisoner who tested positive for HIV was taken out of the general prison population and confined to a hospital ward. If they had AIDS, they were further confined to a room, isolated from any human contact. It was solitary confinement for illness, not behavior. The crime they had committed was immaterial. AIDS conferred a death sentence with no reprieve.

When Luke first went to see the slight man who had been signed over to his care, he was in a private room with a prison guard sitting outside the door. Luke walked into the dark space that held a bed and a night table. The shades were drawn. There was a noticeable odor, a sickening combination of sweat and a strange body odor he associated with AIDS. Though the temperature in the room was uncomfortably high, and the patient was covered with a pile of blankets, he was shaking with chills. He coughed in spasms.

Doc, can you stop these chills? His words were barely audible through his chattering teeth.

It hurts so bad. Can you help me?

I will give you a shot for the pain and some medicine to bring your fever down. He put his stethoscope on the skeletal chest, pushing firmly to make a seal over the protruding rib cage. He listened to the heart sounds and feathery breathing, then stood back and looked at the man lying on his side in a fetal position, shaking uncontrollably. On the bedside table was a plastic basin that held several cans of a protein supplement, bobbing in the half-melted ice.

He offered a few reassuring words, but got only a frightened, distant look in response. He stopped at the nursing station and spoke to the patient's nurse. Does anybody come to look in on him? Does he get mail?

No mail. No visitors. They wouldn't be allowed anyway because he's in custody.

So who does he talk to?

Only me, or whichever nurse is on duty . . . and you. The guards just sit there and look at us suspiciously. They don't even look into the room.

What do we know about this guy? Does he have a family we can call? He's not going to make it for more than a week in my opinion.

There's nothing in his record about a family. He was kind of vague—just told me they were long gone.

Twice a day, Luke returned to see the man. Whatever his crime had been, he was reduced to a shrunken, pathetic shadow. Conversation was difficult, but he tried to say a few words. The man usually just stared vacantly at him. His ghostly face displayed a look of complete despondence mixed with pain. The nurses dutifully changed his sheets, gave him bed baths, and brought him meals. Otherwise, he lay there, as alone as anyone could be. As he faded in and out of sleep, he must have known his life was coming to an end. He had no friends or family to talk to, and was unable to express whatever feelings he had with Luke or the nurses. Five days later, he died.

Luke thought of his patient with hemophilia who had contracted AIDS from infected blood. His wife, who was highly educated, had taken a low-level secretarial job with the state so she could get health insurance for them. She said she would scrub floors or do whatever it took. Any job she sought would be solely because they needed health insurance, not because of her talent or interests. They, too, seemed resigned to their fate. The remaining months of his life were consumed with efforts to pay medical bills and maintain some semblance of dignity in a world that had cast them aside.

There were more prisoners, more gay men, a fraternity member from the local college who contracted HIV from a prostitute in Miami, a closeted gay professor who had been infected in Haiti, and many more. The number of those suffering and dying had been mounting, higher and higher over the past year. Luke had watched the scourge of AIDS and the suffering it wrought. He counted himself among those whose lives were touched now almost daily by this vicious pathogen. He saw the telltale purple blotches of Kaposi's sarcoma on their skin, stigmata that foretold their imminent death. He saw them waste away from inanition, the flesh melting off their bones until all that remained was a skeleton draped with sagging skin. He tried every trick he knew to help their breathing, but the Cryptococcus, Histoplasma, and Aspergillus infections continued relentlessly to destroy their lungs.

He often stayed at the hospital so late that he walked through the shadowy parking lot, hearing only the rustle of palm trees. The darkness permeated his soul. He knew that at a time, he had felt one with his surroundings, enveloped in the comforting cocoon of late spring. Now he just felt alone and hopeless.

Chapter 11

June 1987 (Medical Practice—Year Ten)

The days and weeks went by at an exhausting pace. Luke was locked into a relentless pattern. Whether it was or wasn't his own doing did not matter anymore. He had long since decided not to say no when a potential new patient called. He had taken the medical director position at the Cluster out of concern for these beings—yes, human beings—who existed on society's margin, ignored at best, and otherwise feared because of their deformities. He oversaw one hundred patients at a local nursing home, most of whom had no families. They were out of sight and out of mind to the rest of the world rushing past their door.

Nights on call at the hospital—being awakened by the ICU nurse to adjust ventilator settings, order potassium, manage a new fever, or handle scores of other problems—became a slow torture. This was the practice of medicine, his choice. He saw no way out, so he kept going.

There was a time when the constant demands on him, the waves of sickness and dying day and night, were interrupted by levity, though usually only briefly.

Back in his office on another steamy afternoon, he walked from his personal office in the rear and into the hall. The sight he beheld erased his morbid thoughts, if temporarily. Tammie was leading a new patient toward an exam room.

Sam, you can wait in here for the doctor.

Luke watched from a distance as the tall, skinny, unkempt man manipulated his crutches and kept up a steady stream of chatter. He wore unlaced, worn-out boots, a rumpled flannel shirt, and baggy, khaki pants; all filthy. Luke ducked back into his office and heard the patient ask to use the restroom. After twenty minutes of rustling sounds from behind the closed door, Tammie detected the smell of marijuana. She discreetly knocked on the door and called his name.

Mr. Jones? Sam?

Can't a man have some privacy? the patient shouted. You gotta keep track of my time, me doin' my own business?

Luke was summoned and knocked on the door.

Mr. Jones, just for the record, smoking anything in this office is forbidden.

I ain't doin' nuthin', but yessuh, it's your word, and I'll do what the doctor says, all right.

Tammie ushered Mr. Jones into an exam room.

She emerged with a twisted face.

That guy smells awful. Oh, by the way, as I walked away from the room, I heard a lot of racket. The faucets were going on and off, paper towels being pulled from the dispenser, moaning sounds, a cabinet door slamming. I don't know what's happening in there.

Luke grabbed the medical chart and walked in. A foul-smelling cloud hung in the air. The stench caught his breath. The man sat with his pant legs rolled up. Dirty paper towels were scattered by his feet.

What's going on here?

Well, Doc, my feet was dirty, so I thought I'd wash 'em up 'fore you came in. His wet, worn socks lay in a soggy, malodorous heap on the floor next to his boots. The cracked leather was soaked through. He didn't seem to notice.

I see you were in the emergency room over the weekend. Did they refer you here?

Yeah, Doc. Sho did.

You're two hours late for your appointment.

Yeah, be runnin' a little late, look like.

How'd you end up in the ER?

Well, I be passin' through town and got myself into a disagreement. I spit in a feller's face and the cops come and arrested me. They let me out on personal 'cognizance, tol' me I had to come for a trial. Dint have no place to stay, so I slep' on the ground past three nights.

Why didn't you go to the Salvation Army shelter?

The man looked directly into Luke's eyes with a serious expression.

Doc, I pays my own way.

Luke saw no need to pursue it. The man made no sense. Why he was in the emergency room remained a puzzle. His bare feet were cold and mottled and he had open sores between his toes.

What happened to your feet?

Oh, they been givin' me trouble right smart. Seem like theys always cold 'n sore.

Luke changed the topic, curious to figure out what the guy was doing in his office, trying to get some idea of his medical problems and whatever else ailed him. More to amuse himself than anything, he asked, What do you do for a living?

Oh, I repairs typewriters. Axtually, I can purty near fix almost anythin'. Jis waitin' for my feet to git better 'fore I starts back lookin' for work fixin' typewriters.

Luke jokingly continued, Do you plan to pay your medical bill?

Oh, yessuh. I ain't got no money now, but when I gits back to work, I sure will. Yessuh. I know you studied real hard in school and deserves to be paid.

Doc, (with barely a pause) you think drinkin' a little beer will hurt my feet gittin' well?

How can you afford beer if you have no money?

Jis' axin' for when I get back to makin' money.

Found me a room.

Good. Try to get yourself some clean socks and dry shoes. Then, when you get back to your room, soak your feet in warm water and keep them dry. They'll heal up fine.

Doc, ya know, I'm a flute and saxophone player, too. You looks like a saxophone player yo'self.

It was obvious that further conversation wouldn't lead to any better understanding of the man's condition. Luke got up to leave.

Say Doc, you think I need these here crutches?

Only if you can't stand up or walk without them. Looks like you can walk just fine.

Say Doc, you got any pain medicine?

Luke left the room and returned with a dispenser filled with Tylenol samples, each individually wrapped. The man tore open a couple of packets and tossed the pills into his mouth. Then he pocketed a handful of packets and hobbled out, holding the crutches under his arm, not using them to support himself. He didn't bother to say thanks or good-bye.

Luke shook his head. In the past, he would have laughed about such characters that broke up the office monotony. Not anymore. His sense of humor had sustained him for years—macabre, vulgar, politically incorrect inside jokes shared with doctors and nurses as a way to relieve the pressure, to mitigate the unrelenting burden of patients teetering on the brink of life and death.

Now the humor was gone.

Once again his dark mood crept in as he sat staring out the window. The intercom buzzed.

Luke, Mr. Dillard is in Room Two.

He straightened his tie and walked in.

Hello, Henry. You're looking good.

Thanks, Doc. I feel great—thanks to you.

Henry was a big man with a blond shock of hair, pure country in his cowboy shirt and farm jeans.

I did all the rehab, and the heart doctor released me. He said you could take it from here. Tell you the truth, Doc. I'd rather see you anyway. That guy wasn't very sociable. I'm sure he knows his business, but he just didn't talk much.

Well, Henry. I'm glad you're back here, too. You had a pretty bad heart attack and recovered very nicely. Tough to keep a good man down.

Doc, I feel like I got a new lease on life. I quit smokin', but I ain't too good at watching my diet. Henry smiled broadly.

You know what I did, Doc?

No, Henry. Tell me.

Remember in the hospital when I said if I get better I'm gonna get me a new truck?

Yeah, I do remember that, Henry.

The patient beamed.

Well, I got me a brand new F-150, candy-apple red. She's parked right outside and she's a beauty. So, thanks again Doc. Don't know what else to say.

I'm just happy to be alive.

Luke listened to Henry's heart and they chatted for a few more minutes, then said good-bye. He went back to his office and thought about Henry. He felt flattered at Henry's gratitude, but knew that he would have only a partial reprieve. His heart had been damaged badly. He was happy that Henry felt good and hoped he could enjoy the new pickup truck that was his dream come true.

The office continued to be busy with patients waiting to be seen, when Luke was interrupted by a call from the emergency room. The day was unbearably hot as he walked across the street to the hospital. He felt sticky all over with sweat and was met by a shock of cold air as he opened the door, swiped his card so the hospital operator knew he was there, and walked down the hall.

Mary, one of his patients from the Cluster—the only one with a regular visitor—had been delivered to the hospital by ambulance after she had a grand mal seizure. He told the ER nurse to send her directly to the ICU. He walked in through the swinging doors and over to the glassed-in cubicle. She lay there, a small, twisted figure, dwarfed beneath the sheets and bathed in perspiration. Her breathing was fast and labored. Her elderly mother, quiet as always, sat next to the bed holding Mary's shriveled hand in her own. Her eyes reflected terror.

He picked up the chest X-ray from the table

that accompanied her from the ER and popped it onto the screen. Her thorax was hopelessly contorted from scoliosis, making it difficult to see her lungs alongside the shadow of her heart and spine. After a few seconds, the diagnosis was obvious to him. She had no doubt vomited and aspirated fluid into her lungs, setting up a raging chemical reaction that would soon develop into pneumonia if she lived long enough for the bacteria to begin their assault. In her case, the stomach acid caused such a severe outpouring of fluid into her lungs that any chance to save her was infinitesimal. No wonder it was referred to as shock lung.

He examined her as best he could. She shuddered at any human touch and looked at him with a frightened, if vacant stare. Her gown was soaked through. He winced at her body odor. He knew she would not survive unless her breathing was supported by a ventilator.

Her mother shrank into herself with fear. She knew what was coming. The expression on her face gave away her thoughts. He knew her daughter was her life. He had become aware of that over time, as he'd seen her week after week, sitting silently next to Mary at the Cluster, clutching her gnarled hand.

Luke took her into a small conference room, closed the door and sat down next to her.

I think you understand how serious Mary's condition is.

She nodded.

I'm afraid the only way we can keep her alive is to put a tube down her windpipe and support her breathing with a machine called a ventilator.

He hesitated.

Unfortunately, because of her severe medical problems, the chance that we would ever be able to get her off the machine is close to zero.

She looked up. Her voice was quiet and steady.

How long would she live on the machine?

Luke knew she would die with or without the ventilator. Now it was time to prepare her mother for that fact.

It depends on what complications might occur. She would need antibiotics, and most likely medicine to support her blood pressure. We would have to keep her asleep, so she wouldn't fight the breathing machine. He hesitated.

Even with all that, she would likely not survive another week.

Tears filled her eyes. How long would she live without the machine?

Probably a day or two, at most.

I don't want her to suffer. The Lord knows she has had such a hard life and has suffered so long. She is my little angel. I can't stand the thought of her being gone, but I knew the day would come.

She wiped her eyes, composed herself.

Can you make her comfortable, maybe help

her sleep? And can I stay with her?

Yes, I will make sure she is sleeping comfortably, and I'll give her something to bring her temperature down. You can be at her side as long as you like.

He patted her shoulder, paused for a few seconds, then left the room.

He walked out and wrote the order—DNR. Do not resuscitate. It was cold, clear and succinct. For a fleeting moment he contemplated how simple it was to end a life. He thought of himself writing an order for a death sentence. He knew her death was imminent. Nothing could stop it. He still felt like it was somehow his doing. He was the last line of defense and felt he had failed her. He tried to wipe away the self-imposed guilt.

When he related the decision to Mary's ICU nurse, she reacted with a look of relief and sympathy. Her eyes told him she was in agreement. He sensed she was grateful that he had had the courage to be honest with Mary's mother. How many times had she cared for terminal patients when no one was willing to admit the futility of continued treatment? It was always the nurse who was left to spend those last dreadful hours, days and nights, doing her best to provide care, following the orders of a doctor who distracted himself somewhere else.

He knew he had the authority to use his professional judgment in counseling Mary's mother.

He was deeply aware that the words he used to comfort her could sway her decision on behalf of her daughter. Many hundreds of times he had done the same thing, having weighed all the variables, concluding that any more treatment would be futile. Then, armed with his conclusion, he had faced a mother, father, son, or daughter. Sometimes he'd stood in the waiting room and spoken to a group of extended family huddled around him, hanging on every word.

Though it hurt the family greatly to hear the short speech, for him it had become easy to give. He hoped he did not sound uncaring. He was confident when he advised a family that the situation was hopeless. It was easy to write the DNR order. It was even easy, if uncomfortable, to have a family say, *Do everything, Doc. That's what she would want. She's a fighter.*

The decision belonged to them. He became the instrument.

Nevertheless, when he heard *do everything*, he foresaw the horrific experience of the ensuing days or weeks:

catheters

IV fluids

needle punctures

bleeding and swelling from infiltrated IV sites

ventilator settings managed day and night

endotracheal tube sagging along the side of the comatose patient's mouth green oxygen prongs sticking up the nostrils

sometimes a gastric tube for feeding through the stomach wall

diarrhea

falling blood pressure,

endless rounds of antibiotics, cardiac drug,

countless blood tests

transfusions to replace the blood withdrawn for endless tests

And all for what? To prolong "life." He thought again about the no-man's-land between life and death. A patient in a coma with no chance of recovery was not the same as a fully conscious person struggling to survive from bleeding to death after a car accident or a gunshot wound. The terror he had seen in the eyes of a man gasping for breath, begging for life, was entirely different. It spoke in his mind to the apparent innate need to survive at all costs. It was an unquestioned need, without which life would have little value.

Technically, the comatose, terminally ill patient was likewise alive. Then, when the heart stopped beating and the pupils became fixed and dilated, all of a sudden it was obvious that life had ended and death had taken over.

Talking to a family decision-maker about a hopeless situation, then writing the order to stop treatment that would only prolong the inevitable was not hard for him, because he was convinced it was the right thing to do. However, he could do only as directed by the family—whether they assented to his suggestion to stop treatment or directed him to keep up life-prolonging measures. Why they were called "heroic" measures escaped him. At best, they were a routine part of the job. At worst, if he did not suffer the discomfort of being honest with the family, those fruitless measures could be a cowardly way to avoid the fact of the matter. Death was on its way.

Yet it was hard—the two sides of a coin. It was hard to see the pain in their eyes when reality struck like a bolt of lightning. Up to that very minute, the family and the patient had lived for months and years in some kind of rhythmic harmony, often in deep denial. Suddenly, in a few seconds, they were forced to face the truth of the patient's mortality. For them it was as though the earth stopped turning. They were turned upside down by fear and grief. And each time he shared those words, *There is nothing more we can do to keep her alive,* he shared their grief in a small way.

There was a time when he hadn't been so philosophical about it. Now those conversations seemed to come more often. He kept a game face now, but each was another painful stab. He was the doctor.

His patients had all been rescheduled, so he drove home. The good feelings he had about Sam and Henry dissipated like a puff of smoke.

Mary died the following day.

Chapter 12

July 1987 (Medical Practice—Year Ten)

The courtroom was silent except for the occasional cough or creak of the benches as the spectators shifted in their seats. The jurors filed in and seated themselves in two orderly rows. As the judge swept through a side door, arranged his robe, and took his place, everyone rose, then sat down.

The defense attorney began to lay out his case. The night nurse was called to the stand. He allowed her to testify that the doctor was diligent and caring. Did he see the deceased on a regular basis? Did he examine her and provide direction on how to care for her wounds? All her responses were supportive.

Then the plaintiff's attorney stood up and walked toward her, positioning himself so he could pose questions to her while catching the eye of the jury. His questions were designed to tie her in knots.

You have testified that the doctor was conscientious and attentive to the deceased, is that correct?

Yes.

He grilled her with details so granular that they seemed unrelated to the case.

Did he remove the dressings on her wound each time he saw her? Did he comment on the smell? Did he ever make statements about whether she would be better off dead than lying semi-comatose in a bed with a feeding tube and deep infections on her backside? Did he always answer his pages? How often did he come to the nursing home? Was it the same time each month?

The questions came in a staccato voice, almost randomly. It was obvious he was attempting to trip her up, to find inconsistency in her answers in order to create doubt in the jurors' minds about her credibility. She held her head high and tried to remain calm, but her voice quaked. He continued to probe her, trying to get her to contradict herself. She was weakened but not broken when she left the witness box, nearly in tears. She had tried to paint a picture of sympathy for the doctor and his decisions.

The defense attorney had done his best to provide testimony in support of Luke. But as he sat and listened, Luke felt like words were left hanging in the air, making the phrases and sentences seem disjointed. The jury had long since zoned out. It seemed to him that all they were focused on was the fact of an old woman's death—at his hand. She was alive, then dead; no return. And if they somehow believed he could have and should have kept her alive at all cost, they would hold him accountable. He felt the blood drain from his body as panic welled up within him. He was frozen to the chair.

He snapped to the present and felt a faint glimmer of hope as the defense attorney called his expert witness to the stand. Over the next thirty interminable minutes, the entire story was again played out. The expert was calm and credible, and supportive of Luke's decision to allow his patient, whose condition was futile, to die with a modicum of peace and dignity.

Then it was the plaintiff attorney's turn. He pounded away at the expert, repeatedly trying to convince the jury that the patient had been allowed to die unnecessarily, that she died because of callous disregard by the doctor whose responsibility it was to fulfill his Hippocratic Oath to keep his patients alive.

He probed deeper, again and again, in an effort to impugn the credibility of the expert.

Is it customary for doctors to let their patients die without the benefit of antibiotics and other life-saving measures?

It depends on the circumstances.

The plaintiff's attorney cut him off.

Oh, so if it is inconvenient to intervene because

it's the middle of the night, and it's a patient who is not surrounded by her family demanding care, it's OK to let her die?

I did not say that or imply it.

The expert's voice rose with confident indignation.

Under extreme circumstances it may be medically and ethically acceptable to refrain from trying to keep a patient alive at all costs.

The attorney spoke slowly.

Doctor, we are not talking hypothetically here. This was an elderly woman lying defenseless with no family around her to demand help.

His voice rose to an indignant crescendo.

Is this way of handling a dying patient something that occurs frequently, or is this just the way the defendant has chosen to practice?

He stabbed his finger toward Luke as he spoke.

The defense attorney jumped to his feet and exclaimed, Objection, your honor! Badgering the witness!

Objection sustained. You may answer if you wish.

The expert paused, then spoke slowly in a shaky voice of barely controlled anger.

Every doctor . . . who practices primary care medicine . . . faces this situation at some time in their career.

The plaintiff's attorney wheeled around as if to discount the comment.

No further questions, Your Honor.

The jury listened. Their emotions were unreadable.

Then it was Luke's turn. He had insisted on testifying in his own defense, despite objections from his lawyer.

You are taking a big chance. The plaintiff's attorney will try to lead you to contradict yourself. Let the jury decide based on the case we've laid out.

He would not be swayed. He could not do it any other way, sitting powerless while others argued for and against his medical decision. There was no chance he would remain mute while the plaintiff's attorney fabricated a story designed to blame him, to make him out to be a heartless killer. He knew he alone was accountable and needed to defend himself. He was called to the witness stand.

He rose to his feet, stood straight, walked over to the witness stand and sat. The sleepless night had had no effect on him. His mind was acute. Over many years he had dragged himself to the hospital in a half-awake state, only to have his brain snap to attention as he confronted a dying patient. This day felt no different. He arranged the microphone, raised his right hand and swore to tell the truth.

The plaintiff, the deceased patient's son, sat directly in front of him, next to the attorney. Luke had never seen nor spoken to the son, who sat hunched over the table with his meaty hands crossed, appearing uncomfortable in his ill-fitting brown suit and floral tie. In fact, Luke had not heard from any family member or even a friend, for that matter. Luke tried to hide his reflexive disgust for the man.

He tried to remain serious and confident as he nodded slightly to the jury, then locked his eyes on the defense attorney as he rose from his chair.

Doctor, could you please describe your education, training, and medical practice experience?

He had rehearsed his answer many times. He had told himself to keep it simple, clear and straightforward. *Speak slowly. Look at the jury as though you are talking to them. They need to know who you are.* He was self-conscious, almost embarrassed. *How*, he thought, *do you recite the names of medical school, residency training, and fellowships without sounding pompous?* Most of these people are simple country folk. *Just go ahead and say it,* he thought, and he did. *They can think what they want.* The direct testimony was meant to be thorough, but not drawn out.

Please tell the court about your patient.

I am the medical director of the nursing home where she resided and where I personally care for about a hundred of the hundred and forty residents. All of them are medically complicated. All of them had been transferred to my care because their doctors were not willing to see them at the nursing home. They likened it to making house calls, which they were unwilling to do.

He continued to paint a verbal picture to get the jury to understand the horrible physical and mental state of these elderly people. The nursing home stood on a well-traveled street, with the ebb and flow of traffic passing before it day and night. No one gave it a sideways glance as they sped by. It was rare for anyone to walk through those doors. When they did, the awful smell of stale urine set off an olfactory shock.

Most of the residents slumbered or lay half-awake staring into space. Once or twice a day, they were laboriously untangled from the bed and positioned in a wheelchair. The chairs were lined up in a row, each patient tethered by yellow restraints that held them in the chair. Gradually they would slump over asleep, heads bent to the side, slack bodies supported by the restraint. Some were able to move about slowly, using their feet to propel the chair forward in random directions. Eventually the nursing staff would find time to wheel them back and return them to bed. The process was so cumbersome and time-consuming that the over-worked staff struggled to stay on schedule.

How long have you been responsible for these nursing home patients?

I was asked to provide care for them about six months ago because it became clear to the nursing home director that individual doctors rarely came to see their patients according to a schedule required by Medicare. Virtually all their care was directed by telephone. I agreed to visit them regularly, so I took over their management.

Did all the descriptions you have given about the condition of these patients exist when you assumed their care?

Yes. I wrote orders to increase their activity wherever possible, dress their wounds properly, culture their urine if I suspected an infection, and do many other things to try to improve their condition.

Can you describe the condition of the elderly lady, Lucille Cartwright, who passed away and is the subject of this lawsuit?

Luke paused, then began to summarize the story.

In many ways she was like most of the other patients in the nursing home. She had been transferred to my care six months before she died. When I first saw her, she was semicomatose and unable to communicate. When she was awake, she did not recognize the nurses or me. She had multiple contractures and was severely emaciated. She had deep bedsores that were cleaned and packed daily with large amounts of gauze. They had been there a long time, and there was no chance they would heal. The cavities were open down to the sacral and hip bones. The nursing staff would raise her up in bed and try to feed her, but it was a tedious process and much of the food dribbled out of her mouth. They worked very hard at providing her adequate nutrition, but it was impossible, so they had to resort to tube feeding.

Did she have visitors?

No, I never saw anyone visit her. I tried to find family members to discuss her care. We had one contact name. The nurses called whoever-it-was and were told not to bother them. There was no address.

He went on to describe her final hours.

She drifted into a coma and her temperature rose. Her breathing became shallow and labored. When I was called, I told the nurses to keep her comfortable. I was certain she had developed pneumonia from aspirating food into her airways. I believed it would be fruitless and inhumane to send her to the hospital where she would receive all the care guaranteed to a dying patient. He recited the litany: blood tests, X-rays, ventilator dependency, intravenous fluids, a nasogastric tube for feeding, drugs to raise her blood pressure, antibiotics for her pneumonia and infected bedsores, a Foley catheter to monitor urine output, and much more.

What he wanted to say was, And all this would be done in a futile attempt to prolong her life without consideration of her pain and suffering, and the fact that she was a dying woman. Why? Because life at all costs is always considered better than no life. And death is irreversible.

Instead, he told the court that he had asked the

nurses to try once more to reach the family. They did, and later told him that no one answered the phone. He explained that he felt the ethical and humane decision was to keep her at the nursing home where she would die peacefully. Four hours later she was dead.

Thank you, Doctor.

The defense attorney looked at the judge.

That's all I have, your honor.

The courtroom remained quiet for a moment. The plaintiff's attorney made a show of scraping the floor with his chair as he pushed back from the table, breaking the silence. He stood facing the witness stand and affected a look of incredulity. He ignored any reference to empathy for the dying patient. Instead, he stabbed directly.

Doctor, did you have instruction from your patient or her family representatives to withhold medical care?

No.

Did she have a Living Will or leave any instructions to withhold heroic measures?

No, I ...

The attorney interrupted to emphasize his indignation, then raised his voice.

So, you decided to play God and let this lady die without antibiotics and hospital care. Without communicating with her family. Without allowing her family to decide what would be best for her?

Anger welled up like a volcano erupting

inside, but Luke had prepared himself for the accusation. He took a breath. His voice was only a little unsteady.

I had never seen her family. As far as I know, no one called about her condition over the months since I had assumed responsibility for her care. The night she died the nurses had repeatedly called the only number they had and got no answer.

The plaintiff's attorney pounced.

Did you personally ever try to contact a family member?

No, I did not personally dial the phone. I would have spoken with the family had the nursing staff told me who they were and how I might reach them.

So, you personally made no call, is that right?

Yes, that is correct.

The attorney continued his effort to discredit Luke.

So you made the decision to let her die?

I made the decision…

Doctor, I asked you a question. Did you make the decision to let her die? Yes or no.

The defense attorney stood.

Objection your honor! He is not allowing the doctor to explain his answer.

The judge said, Sustained. You may answer.

Luke faced the jury.

I made the decision to withhold aggressive care because Mrs. Cartwright had extensive medical problems that could not be cured. She was emaciated, could not eat, had severe contractures of her arms and legs, and was bedridden. She had deep, infected bedsores and had developed pneumonia. And she had dementia and could not speak, understand, or recognize anyone.

He sensed a subtle quake in his voice as he finished his explanation.

The plaintiff's attorney looked at him and addressed him with a sarcastic tone.

Are you finished?

He thought for a second.

No, I am not.

The attorney looked surprised and jerked his head toward the judge, whose expression made it clear he would allow the doctor to comment further.

Luke turned and looked directly at the jury, then spoke.

As a physician I have spent my career trying to improve the health of my patients. I work hard to make the correct diagnosis, using my medical skills and the best available technology to make a diagnosis. Then I treat them the best way I know how in order to make them better. Sometimes there is no treatment. Sometimes all the technology in the world cannot keep a person alive when their time has come. If that is the case, I am honest about it. If a patient has terminal cancer, I explain the situation. Sometimes they demand treatment because they feel anything is better than nothing. But most of the time they grow to accept the inevitability of their death. My job, then, is to comfort them, to support them, to provide pain relief.

Mrs. Cartwright was terminally ill. I was unable to talk to her because of her dementia. Her family was unavailable to discuss her situation. When I was called that night I knew that keeping her alive with IVs, ventilators, cardiac monitors, and antibiotics would not make her well. Her medical problems were so far advanced there was nothing more that could have been done to improve her health or lessen her discomfort. Her time had come and I, as her physician, had the ethical responsibility to allow her to die peacefully. Sometimes that is the job of a physician. It is never easy. It is never pleasant. But it is the right thing to do.

He stopped talking and looked down.

The attorney spoke in an impatient tone.

Are you finished?

Luke responded softly.

Yes.

Doctor, do you need to contact a patient's family every time there is a need for immediate treatment when the patient is incapacitated?

Whenever possible, yes.

What if they are unavailable?

Then, if the situation is life-threatening, and if it is appropriate, I will begin treatment.

The attorney jumped in without a pause.

Was Mrs. Cartwright's family available the night you made the decision to let her die?

No. No one answered the phone.

The phone call you did not personally make, but delegated to a nurse. . . . Doctor, did this patient have terminal cancer?

No.

Doctor, is the presence of coma, fever, and infected bedsores always fatal?

Not necessarily.

He heard the strain in his own voice. He knew he was being boxed into a trap. He looked down at the glass of water. Maybe he could pause for a drink of water to regain his composure. But wouldn't that be too obvious? The courtroom seemed so quiet. He felt everyone's eyes glued on him, waiting for him to say something.

The attorney spoke to him as though to a child.

Doctor, you just testified that fever, coma, and infected bedsores are not necessarily irreversible, meaning they are not a death sentence. Doctor, can we agree that death is final?

The defense attorney jumped to his feet. Objection!

Overruled. You may continue.

So, Doctor, let me be clear. If a patient is in a coma, develops a fever, and has infected bedsores, I believe you refer to that condition as sepsis, isn't that correct?

Yes, such a condition would be called sepsis.

And sepsis is not terminal cancer, is it?

No.

OK. And you testified that such a condition is not necessarily irreversible, is that correct?

Yes, but…

Excuse me, Doctor. Please just answer my questions. For clarity's sake. I believe we can all agree that irreversible in this case means death, correct?

Yes.

Then reversible must mean that this condition does not always lead to death, is that correct?

Yes.

Yet, for Mrs. Cartwright, who did not have terminal cancer, there was no second chance since you let her die, is that correct?

You are twisting my comments out of context.

The attorney had turned to face the jury, but then suddenly wheeled around to confront Luke.

Excuse me, Doctor, for your information, the context is that you let Mrs. Cartwright die. You did not contact her loved ones. You did not allow her or anyone representing her to guide your decision. You simply decided, unilaterally, in the middle of the night, to let her die. He repeated himself, slowly and deliberately.

You … let … her … die.

No further questions, your honor.

Luke stepped down from the witness chair and walked heavily to the defense table. His mind was

numb. He heard the words of the closing argu-
ments as an echo reverberating through his skull,
random sounds that seemed like competing
conversations in a foreign language. Then he heard
the judge.

Court is in recess. The jury will begin delibera-
tions immediately.

The judge struck his gavel sharply, stood, and
walked out. First one row, then the other, the jury
left through a side door. The few observers walked
out. The lawyers gathered their papers and stuffed
them into briefcases. Luke dragged himself out of
his chair and walked stiffly out the door. The
encouraging words of his attorney were background noise. He forced a smile. He rode home
with his wife, mostly silent. In his head, he burned
to say something, but the words would not come.
He watched the prairie through the car window.
She parked the car in the yard and walked into the
house. He sat for a few moments and looked at the
house, a beautiful log structure. He thought of the
Lincoln Logs that he had played with as a kid,
stacking them up in a rectangular design. He and
his brother had torn the structures down, then
rebuilt them, hour after hour.

He snapped back to reality and shuffled into
the house, going to his study. He sat in the chair
and loosened his tie. *You let her die.* The closing
words of the prosecuting attorney echoed in his
head. *Yes,* he thought, *I did let her die. Was I wrong? I*

can't undo it. I could have transferred her to the hospital. It would have been so easy to keep treating each failing organ until the blood quit flowing. Death will happen when it is time. No amount of surgery or medicine would have reversed her downhill slide. But at least, then, no one would have said it was my fault. It would not have been my burden to carry. I could easily have hidden behind those empty dismissive words: We did everything we could. I'm so sorry. If the patient had suffered pain from every needle puncture or had gagged every time the airways were suctioned on the way to her death, so be it. The easy way for me would have been to keep treating.

The hard part was saying, *That's enough.*

Isn't that what empathy is? Aren't we taught to synthesize all our medical knowledge, experience, and the individual circumstance, and merge them together to reach the right decision? And that decision sometimes is, No, I will not add to the pain. I will not prolong the agony. Death is part of the continuum.

But the irreversibility haunted him. Yes, he was playing God. He decided when the end would be.

Where did that foolish expression come from? Playing God meant deciding when a patient's life was over. Yes, that is the ultimate decision. But aren't the other decisions about how to treat patients, when to stop treatment, even offering strong recommendations, in some sense, playing God? Medicine is sometimes a craft—sometimes an art. Sure, the technical ability to successfully remove a gall bladder or set a fracture is a skill. It may take time to learn, but distilled to its core, it is a skill, not unlike welding or car repair.

The art of medicine is applied to the question of when to operate, not how to perform a procedure.

We are all guilty of making decisions by gently convincing our patients to do what we feel is best. We develop the skill to metamorphose a recommendation into a decision. Our patients become complicit because they need to believe we are doing the best for them. We may know our decisions are assimilated from imperfect information. They make themselves believe there is no gray area. The natural instinct is to deny that there is uncertainty. Religions were built on the same concept—faith.

Is this playing God? And aren't we damned by a double-edged sword? If my treatment decision is correct, but side effects occur, the blame falls on me. If a patient dies because I make an ethical decision to stop the torment of needless, fruitless, life-prolonging procedures and allow her to die peacefully in her sleep, I am to blame.

I had made an active decision to say, No More. It would have been a passive decision or a non-decision to treat until there was nothing left to treat. Was it fair to the patient to watch her blood pressure continue to fall and listen to the beeping monitor signal her heart slowing down, all the time pushing vasopressors into her veins or applying 400 joules of electrical current to her chest, tattooing it where the round paddles touched her and creating the stench of burning skin, all the while knowing that the outcome would nevertheless be death? Would the attorney have criticized me for playing God if I had given up only when death happened, despite all the fruitless efforts to forestall it? We tried everything. Now are you satisfied?

He wanted to blurt out, Isn't it playing God to self-righteously defend life at all costs, to allow suffering to continue after a person's body has given up the will to live?

He sat and thought about the decision he had made. The one that had landed him in court. He began to second-guess himself. Could someone just once say to him, *You did the right thing?* All he had were his own thoughts. There was no one to give him support for his decision to allow his patient to die peacefully. The critics were right there to condemn him, to pass judgment.

Six hours later the phone rang. It was his attorney.

The jury has reached a decision.

The car ride back to the courthouse was a blur. He walked in robotically and sat in his chair.

The jury sat down, expressionless. Everyone in the courtroom sat in silence. The judge issued the standard question, Ladies and gentlemen of the jury, have you reached a verdict?

The jury captain stood and said, Yes, your honor. We have.

What say you?

We, the jury, find for the defendant.

Luke froze. Then his shoulders dropped and he looked down at the table. He gathered his composure, rose from the chair and offered a weak smile of thanks to his attorney. All he could think of was the closing words of the plaintiff's attorney, *You…let…her…die.*

Chapter 13

July 1987 (Medical Practice—Year Ten)

The case was closed. Luke was off the hook. The jury had decided that his order to allow an elderly, demented person to die did not constitute malpractice.

The courtroom cleared out and he went home. But he could not shed his feelings of doubt about the decision he had made. Though he was vindicated legally, somehow he was unable to escape the pain of those cutting words: *You let her die.*

Luke left the hospital shortly after noon on a Saturday. It was not getting easier. The morning had been crazed, moving from ward to ward, seeing patients, writing notes, counseling families, answering pages. He drove two blocks to University Drive, stopped at the intersection, and turned left. At the end of the block he stopped at a red light—the busiest intersection in town. He waited for the light. He was startled when a college student suddenly appeared and tapped on the window. He opened it.

Excuse me, sir, are you OK?

Indignation welled up.

Yeah, why, what's the problem?

The student recoiled, his face reflecting Luke's brusque tone.

Sorry. I was just wondering because you sat here through a green light.

Oh, I did? I'm so sorry. Must have been preoccupied.

He drove forward at the light change.

What had happened? He knew about blackouts but had never experienced one. He recalled patients with global amnesia, a mild stroke where events for several hours remained a blank. His episode only lasted a minute, and he had not fallen asleep. He could only assume he was preoccupied, distracted by thoughts he could not even identify.

He had said nothing to Betsy, but the stoplight experience signaled something new, and worse. He could not shake the sense of walls closing in on him. He saw himself on the edge of a black abyss, like Edgar Allan Poe's prisoner, tied to the cold floor, feeling the pendulum slowly swinging toward his chest, unable see it, knowing with each arc it was growing closer as the walls pushed him toward a bottomless pit.

He saw no escape, just the steady rhythm.

Every other night, year after year, he was

chained to his pager. He began to lie in bed and watch the phone, waiting for a call. The weight of worry became heavier by the day.

He began to wonder what was normal. His whole life was cancer, heart attacks, strokes, back pain, relentless calls from the ICU, continually being awakened from sleep during nights that seemed unending. His entire life had become a stream of illness. At the grocery store, on the street, at a party, everyone he spoke to or recognized had cancer or diabetes or some chronic illness.

He obsessed about the stoplight episode. Did I black out? Was I that deeply in thought that I could sit through a traffic light?

One Thursday, his day began with a call from a nurse on the medical floor.

Your patient, Leroy Johnson, just expired.

It was not unexpected. Leroy's liver disease had taken its toll. He was bleeding from venipuncture sites; his jaundice was so deep that his skin had taken on a greenish hue. He had been in a coma for two days.

Five minutes later Luke was called from the cardiac unit.

Mr. Woods just passed away.

He had already told the family to expect it. The man's heart was the size of a balloon and had no muscle left to pump the blood. His last days were cruel. He struggled to breathe with his lungs filled with fluid. The morphine provided him a temporary respite. Now he was dead.

Luke followed death from one floor to another. The doors to the ICU swung open and beckoned him to the bedside of a diabetic prisoner who had been found in his cell unconscious two days ago. When he was brought to the hospital, he was brain dead. A flatline EEG. His heart was beating, and a ventilator supported his breathing. The unfortunate man, apparently a drifter, had been jailed many times for nonviolent crimes, most recently, grand larceny. For two days, the hospital social worker uncovered every rock to find his family, with no luck. After a session with the hospital lawyer, the medical examiner, and the prison system, Luke turned off the ventilator.

Three deaths in one day. What else could happen?

Before he left for home in the evening, he stopped to see Paul, a young man who was facing death from cystic fibrosis. Paul had made a decision *not* to allow Luke to support his breathing with a ventilator during yet another episode when he no longer had the strength to breathe on his own. He knew his lungs were shot. With the ventilator, there was no hope to live longer than a few agonizing months, and he was too tired to face it. He would not celebrate his twenty-third birthday.

Luke sat at the nursing station and picked up strains from a Grateful Dead song. Paul had shared his love for the music with Luke, and was now playing it to give them both solace. It was a song called *Black Peter*. The lyrics spoke of dying, the sun shining, and friends coming 'round.

Luke was drawn to the room by the music. He looked into the young man's eyes and saw a resignation.

Are you sure you don't want the ventilator? I am afraid that without it, you won't last through the night.

I know, Doc. We've been over this. I've had enough. I'm not afraid to die. Just give me something to help me sleep.

The words came slowly, muffled by the oxygen mask that hugged his nose and mouth. Whatever family he had was far away. He faced his death alone in the small room. Luke stood at the end of the bed. He felt the dusk outside closing down the light of the day and saw his young patient's life yielding to the darkness.

Good-bye, Paul.

Paul gasped his last words.

Good-bye, Doc. Thanks for trying.

Luke sat in his truck as the streetlights lit up the parking lot. His thoughts went back to the trial. A conversation raged in his head. A voice spoke clearly to him, *I know I keep up with medical advances.* Another voice countered, *Maybe not enough.*

Am I fooling myself? No, that makes no sense.

One voice kept up a mantra, You screwed up. You let that lady die. And you have done it before. Are you playing God? You screwed up. You let her die.

The voice was both trite and pious. And persistent. It was his voice. The other countered, I knew what I was doing. Goddammit, practicing medicine is not like following a cookbook. Maybe that's the problem. If only the decisions could be black and white.

But aren't they? Life and death seem pretty binary. Here today, gone tomorrow.

A debate raged. He felt like an observer of his own mind.

Yes, if you screw up, life becomes death in the snap of a finger. But it's all the complexity in between. You do everything to prevent that switch from flipping because when it flips, there is no going back.

Should everything I do be directed toward stopping the gravitational slide from life to death? Why? Is there a moral code that keeps you on the track? If you work hard at sustaining life, then death will not happen. The patient would be grateful, the family would be happy, and you would feel a sense of relief.

That makes no sense.

The debate raged on.

I lost three patients in one day, and I can add Paul tomorrow. No one would fault me for that. People die.

So, do you feel a sense of accomplishment signing death certificates, or telling families what to expect? Oh, maybe you feel relief that your days of standing watch over those poor souls has ended. Does it give you relief, then, to know that death has taken another load off your shoulders? Or do you feel worse that you can't bring them back to life? After all, your job is to heal the sick.

Chapter 14

August 1987 (Medical Practice — Year Ten)

The routine continued. High blood pressure, back pain, coughs, headaches. The names and faces all blended together. At the hospital, he walked up stairways and down halls, from room to room, visiting his patients. Back at his office, he examined a couple of patients, listened to their complaints, wrote prescriptions, filled out billing statements, and wrote cursory notes in the charts. Then it was back to the hospital at noon and a return to the office through the sweltering heat. The digression was only temporary. He felt panicky and hopeless.

Luke took a deep breath and pulled the chart from the rack. Then he saw the name on the chart and smiled. Even in his dark mood, Elmer Osowski could do that for him. He opened the door, ready to see the little man seated in the chair in his brown suit. Elmer's wife insisted he wear his only suit when he went to the doctor. She would fix his ancient, wide tie in a Windsor knot that was always slightly askew.

He always looked like a fresh-faced little boy, though his gray hair showed his age. Despite his obvious discomfort with the regalia, Elmer followed his wife's orders.

Elmer was not in the chair, but his wife sat in her usual place in the corner, a diminutive sparrow of a woman.

Hello, Mrs. O.

Elmer had insisted that Luke call him by his first name, and in turn Elmer called him "Doc." Luke could not bring himself to call Elmer's wife by her first name, Theresa. Her tidy appearance and kind manner deserved more formality. So, he had settled on "Mrs. O," a compromise they'd both accepted.

She looked up at Luke and dabbed her eyes with a well-used linen handkerchief.

Oh, Doctor. Elmer's not with us anymore. He passed away two weeks ago.

She forced a tiny smile through her tears.

Luke walked over and took her hand, then sat down.

Oh, my God, Mrs. O. I'm so sorry.

He paused for a moment as though his next words were trapped inside him.

Tell me what happened.

She spoke slowly.

You know he was beginning to get confused at

times. So, one evening he was mumbling a little bit and said he was going to bed. I didn't really think anything of it, but I asked him if he was OK. He never complained, and as usual, said he just needed to sleep. He snored something awful, so I had been sleeping in the other bedroom. I went to bed, and the next morning I went into his room. He wasn't snoring at all and I got worried.

She sighed and wiped away a tear.

Doctor, I couldn't wake him up. I called 9-1-1 and the Rescue came within ten minutes. They rushed into his bedroom and after a few minutes came out. They told me he had passed away, probably from a stroke.

Thoughts of Elmer flashed through Luke's brain. He had retired two years before from a steel plant in Pennsylvania and moved with his wife to be near their daughter. Elmer always had an impish grin that showed his small, straight teeth. He kept his hair in a short crew cut, a style he'd had since childhood. Luke recalled Elmer's nervous habit of scratching his head before he talked. Always cheerful, he could not have been happier living where it was warm with the two people he loved the most.

Mrs. O pulled a box of medication samples from her purse and set it on the table.

Doctor, when Elmer told you last year his insurance didn't cover the cholesterol medicine and we couldn't afford it, you gave it to him for free.

Luke remembered that he had cajoled a drug salesman to give him boxes of the medicine, which he'd given to Elmer at each quarterly visit.

There's a lot left here, so I thought someone else could use it.

Mrs. O's thoughtfulness, even in the midst of her sorrow, was so typical of her.

Also, Doctor, I wanted to give you this.

She handed Luke a wooden ballpoint pen.

Elmer made these at home as a hobby, and he'd told me he was almost finished with the one he'd made special for you. He was going to bring it today. The only thing left was the wood burning. He was writing "Doc James" but only finished "Doc." I know he would want you to have it.

Luke thanked her and they both stood. He bent down to hug her. She smiled and said good-bye. He walked into his office, set the pen down in front of him, and sat heavily in the chair.

Another death.

A midafternoon thunderstorm left steam rising from the blistering hot asphalt road as he drove toward home across the prairie. He pulled off the road impulsively and parked the truck near a hiking trail. Maybe a walk could clear his fogged-over brain. The path wandered through a canopy of live oaks and palm trees, dripping from the recent rain shower. The moist ground gave off a primeval, earthy, strangely comforting smell. The cicadas made a deafening noise as they came to life after a summer downpour. He wanted—no, needed—to stop obsessing about death.

His mind took him to another place, an ancient hill town in central Italy that he had visited with Betsy five years before. The land was populated by the Umbrians well over two millennia ago. Over time they'd lived alongside the Etruscans. Both farmed, hunted, raised families, and created a culture over three centuries. They gradually died out as the Roman Empire developed and immersed the remaining inhabitants in a new culture. But not before building a walled city overlooking the Tiber River.

When the Empire fell several hundred years later, its provinces, far and near, slowly disintegrated. Today, all that is left of that walled city overlooking the Tiber is a town of worn and tumbled stone. One can gaze upon the consecutive sets of walls and arches, and at the ruins of churches and other buildings along the ancient cobbled streets. To touch the cold rock evokes thoughts of an imponderable history, the only witnesses to which are the stone skeletons.

He took his thoughts further. What is life, then, but an infinitesimal speck? All the hopes and fears, laughter and tears, births and deaths, struggles and victories, and bleeding and dying passed in an instant of history. The life of one individual seen in light of countless millions seems so transient and meaningless. Didn't Stalin once say that a single killing is painful to watch, while murdering by the thousands is easy? Life, then death. Poets and writers try to explain it all, but to what end? The value of a single life in the context of history seems so irrelevant.

He found himself back at the truck, no better off for his meandering thoughts. He recalled that Hannah Arendt had characterized Eichmann's behavior during the Holocaust as the "banality of evil." *But isn't an individual life that becomes death, like flipping off a switch, itself banal?* Try as he might, his mind kept returning to the thought.

Maybe he needed counseling . . . but by whom? One of the psychiatrists he knew from his medical practice? The one who was having an affair? The one who had been in rehab for drug abuse? To his mind, they were all like him—flawed and confused. How could he expect any insight from therapists who continued to grapple with their own demons? They shared the same conundrum as he.

Thoughts of his family intruded: I have a loving wife and a young daughter. Isn't that what holds me to this life? But I am not being fair to them with my obsessions. My entire existence is consumed with the responsibilities of caring for this unending crush of dying patients. I have no energy left to focus on the needs of my family.

Betsy and Lucy deserved something better than a father and husband who had lost his ability to compartmentalize, to keep at bay the mental anguish he carried home every night. His hold on reality continued to slip away.

He maintained a thin veneer of control as he drove home. A strange sense of calm began to grow. He knew what he had to do. Dinner that evening was predictable. He pushed his food around the plate and made small talk. Lucy left the table to play in her room before bedtime. It was all background noise. He helped clear the table and went to his desk. Then, while Betsy was still washing the dishes, he returned to the kitchen.

Oh, crap. I just got a call. I have to go back to the hospital to see a patient. To the referring doctors, it's always urgent, though it never really is.

He barely looked up and feigned a cavalier shrug. Business as usual. He gave her a quick kiss and walked toward the door.

See you later.

He tried to make it sound true. It took all his energy to say the three words. He thought he might have overacted the part, but rushed out, half-embarrassed.

It was dusk and the late-evening, summer breeze caused the palm trees to sway with their papery sound. He drove across the prairie in a trance. Anyone on the street would have seen the doctor, driving slowly in the traffic, looking like any other middle-aged man, focused on where he was going. He felt nothing. The strange serenity he'd found grew out of that nothingness. He did not drive to the hospital.

Instead, he turned left toward the university, and into the parking lot at University Field. He parked and looked up at the football stadium that loomed ominously in front of him. He sat in the truck for a minute, scrawled a few words on a page from his small notebook and laid it on the seat. He took off his pager, which made him feel a little naked. He was never more than an arm's length from it—the ball and chain he'd come to accept. He slid out, closed the door and noticed its muted slam, a sound distinct from the night noises that wafted from the street. Car lights played against the palm trees that lined the parking lot. He methodically locked the door and dropped the keys into his pocket.

He looked up again and envisioned the parking lot filled with cars and people on a football Saturday in the fall. Thousands of fans, streaming into the stadium for the game, could be seen from the street as he drove by, invariably on his way to the hospital. This night, he walked directly to Gate H. It was closed, but he knew the chain was loose. He had squeezed through the gate many times to run up and down the stadium steps for exercise

His footsteps echoed as he walked through the tunnel. When he reached the opening to the stands, he stopped and looked out at the silent, unlit football field. Once again he saw a stadium filled with shouting fans on a hot autumn Saturday, eighty thousand of them roaring at the small figures on the field. He was part of that crowd long ago, but it was no longer for him. He turned and looked up. From the many times he had run those steps, he knew there were exactly sixty rows of seats to the top. On those nights he'd gasped for breath as he'd run, feeling the burn in his thighs as he'd beaten himself into physical shape. That, too, seemed long ago.

Being there was like a dream. This night, he didn't hear his breathing, only his steps—slow, rhythmic. He was a zombie, plodding up and up, row after row. His mind played the thought over and over: *You let her die.*

He could not erase the tape. Any other thought was crowded out by the horrible, repetitive mantra.

He reached the top and walked the short distance to the wall. It stood somewhat higher than five feet. He looked over it at the tops of trees, to the street far below. The lights along University Drive bathed the row of royal palms in a mystical light. The wind was like a cool breath. He looked across the street at the string of restaurants, bars, bookstores, and clothing shops. At one time or another, he'd been in all of them. They looked like cardboard facades.

He did not pause. He raised himself up easily, threw one leg up, and rolled to the top onto the cool concrete. The war in his head continued to rage.

Why didn't you save that old woman? You could have tried harder.

No, I did the best I could.

You can't bring her back to life. She is dead.

Death is final.

His brain was cloudy and his thoughts seemed to shout at him from different directions. The words mixed and blended and became an intolerable noise that he could not turn off. *Just get me away; let me escape.* His hands went to his head and he began to mumble.

Death meant nothing; he had seen so much of it. A person would talk, bubbling over with a lifetime of stories, crying tears of sadness or joy, laughing. Then the lights went out. The patient became a doll. The only life remaining was in the memories of friends and loved ones. Tonight he knew what he had to do. It was time.

He had to get out. He had thought over all the possibilities. A drug overdose made no sense. Which drugs? How much to take? Where to get them? He could not write narcotic prescriptions for himself. Carbon monoxide poisoning? He had no garage. What he did know was that the lights went out and it was over. He had seen it so many times—alive, then gone. He had to do it—now. The noise in his head had to stop.

His idea was not unique. He recalled a Sunday morning when he was twelve years old. He had overheard his father, a physician, tell his mother that a colleague had just hanged himself in his basement. It was not the only time a doctor had committed suicide. He'd asked his father why.

His father had responded, casually, *I guess he was tired of living.*

Until now he had never understood what that meant.

He was ready. Just roll over. One turn and it would be over. One quick move, no chance to second-guess.

Just roll off, the voice told him. *You won't have to think about all those ghosts anymore.* He eased closer. The soft wind shifted toward him at that instant. It carried conversation, mostly unintelligible, from across the street. Just then the excited happy squeal of a child floated on the breeze, *Daddy, thank you!*

He glanced across the street and saw the little girl on the sidewalk outside the ice-cream parlor, clutching her father's hand and holding an ice-cream cone. His jumbled thoughts, the cold ledge, the sounds—all blurred as one.

Then he rolled over—off the ledge.

An electrical shock went through him as his body lurched and he fell. He found himself lying against the top row of seats. He had fallen back into the stands.

When he realized he was alive, he curled into a ball and wept uncontrollably. His muscles tightened and his body was racked with spasms as the tears flowed like an open faucet. He cried without self-consciousness, as all the emotion exploded from him, as all the pain and despondence escaped into the summer night.

He choked out a few fractured words.

My little daughter Lucy. Betsy. How could I leave them?

He held his knees to his chest and thought of himself on a string, being whirled in a circle. The velocity became swifter and the string became shorter so that centripetal force pulled him ever faster into the maelstrom, the blackness of death. Then, somehow, that innocent sound in the night had made the string break and he'd been flung outward, shot back into life.

Another chance. He chastised himself as the heavy curtain lifted from his confused brain. He looked up at the sky with hyperacute senses, forming thoughts that had eluded him for a long time.

Get a grip, he admonished himself. You cannot allow the world to control you. It's up to you to break out of the vicious cycle that drove you to the edge.

He couldn't say how long he lay there. He began to breathe slowly and deeply, half-asleep, as though a storm had passed. The humid night was solemn and quiet. His breaths became more rhythmic, punctuated by hitching sobs every few seconds. He lay there and listened. He felt totally calm, enveloped in a blanket of security surrounded by the quiet and darkness.

The stars had never looked so bright. He sat up

and wiped the tears from his face. He began to cry in brief spasms, like the distant claps of thunder that follow a dissipating rainstorm.

He stood up slowly and waited for his legs to become steady. Then he walked carefully down the steps, feeling comfort in the solid support beneath his feet. He marveled to himself at the lightness of each step as he squeezed through the chain and made the short walk to his truck.

He sat for some time, collecting himself. He thought again of Betsy and Lucy. He thought of the little girl across the street who had saved his life. From the seat, he picked up the notepaper on which he had scratched a message. All he had written was, *I'm sorry*. He read it out loud, breathed another deep sob, and tore it to shreds.

Chapter 15

January 1988

Luke sat at his desk and opened a letter. It was addressed to him and written longhand in scratchy penmanship. It read:

Dear Dr. James,

You and I have never met, but I wanted to write you this letter before my health fails me. I was a close friend of Lucille Cartwright but had not seen her in a few years, since she got all confused with that Alzheimer's condition and was taken to a nursing home. I live in a small mobile home here in the country, and had no way to travel to see her. I still think of her a lot and miss her, but I will always have the memories.

My niece visited me recently and told

me about you. She saw in the paper where you had been sued for malpractice by Lucille's son. I never liked her people much. They didn't care for her when she lived out here, and I was not surprised when I heard they never visited her at the nursing home.

My niece said she had heard you cared a lot for your patients, and didn't deserve to be sued. I heard over the past year how Lucille was suffering with bedsores and all, and she couldn't communicate any longer. I am sure you did your best for her. And I know she would have agreed. I hope you are doing well. Thank you for caring.

Sincerely, Sarah Breeden

He stood up and walked over to a wall of ceiling-to-floor windows. To the south, twenty floors below, he looked down on a breathtaking view of Tampa Bay. The setting sun reflected its last light on the tall buildings in the distance and created a sparkling diamond effect on the water. He looked west as the sun began dropping like a salmon-colored egg yolk. It always seemed, just before it set completely, to make a sudden jerk, a last gasp, then disappear below the horizon. It gave him a fleeting jolt of sadness as another day ended.

His focus shifted from the fading light on the horizon to the land. There was the Sun Bowl stadium protruding above the palm trees and low concrete block homes that dotted St. Petersburg. He reread the letter with a smile. Its author would never know what it meant to him—she left no return address, perhaps by design.

As he looked out, his eye caught the Salvador Dali Art Museum down the street from the stadium, and he thought of the hours of solace he had spent there. Mrs. Breeden's kind letter reminded him how staring at the dripping, melting clock paintings had begun to help him overcome his haunting thoughts about the duality of life and death. He'd begun to draw away from obsessive thoughts of literal death. Slowly, his mind began to focus on a merge of the finite and infinite, the concrete and the abstract, and to see the fluidity of time.

Lucille Cartwright was still very much alive to her friend—only now in the form of a fond memory.

Dali's paintings were enclosed by frames, but the paintings themselves had no enclosure. The way Dali blended life and death and time with dreams until they became one was comforting. *All One*, Luke mused.

Weren't all his patients enclosed in their individual frames? Yet, weren't they all free of enclosures as their bodies and souls merged, as their lives moved into death?

He was beginning to see a way out of the vortex that had nearly pulled him to the bottom. With the sudden release, he felt when he struck the pavement and found himself alive, he was propelled upward from his drowning state into a new reality.

Luke saw his reflection in the window, the wooden ballpoint pen in the pocket of his shirt. He lifted the pen, read the word "Doc," and remembered Elmer Osowski. Elmer had shown him the stump of his middle finger, which had been partially amputated in a work accident. Elmer had said, *Jeez, Doc, the way I see it? The Lord didn't want me to get in trouble with my hot head, so he cut off my birdie finger so I couldn't flip it no more.*

Luke smiled. A rush of memories came back. All the deaths that had weighed on him had become softened with time. He saw all his deceased patients as ghosts, but they no longer appeared to him as cold, lost lives. Rather they had become living memories that greeted him in his thoughts and offered wordless consolation and strength. He fingered the handmade pen as he stood at the window.

Luke, there is an oncologist on the phone who insists he needs to speak with you.

His administrative assistant stood in the doorway, reflected from the window.

It had been five months since he left his

medical practice. After careful thought he had accepted a position as medical director for a health insurance company. His role was to evaluate new treatments for coverage decisions. The question was simple: was the proposed treatment considered experimental or unproven? If so, it was not considered a covered benefit. Alternatively, if the treatment was considered to be consistent with the current standard of medical care, it would be paid for by insurance.

Though the question was simple, the answer often proved to be thorny and complex. He was grateful to be able to transition his life as a practicing physician to this new world. To enjoy regular, if long hours, in an office building was a great relief. Far away from the hospital and the unrelenting torment of sick and dying patients who depended on him to pull them back from the unknown. A burden had been lifted.

He had been shocked to notice over the past few months that, in a very real sense, his mind had become clear once again. A mental fog had gradually dulled his thinking over many years of worry and sleeplessness. The fog had crept in unnoticed until his dulled senses had accepted it as normal. Now it was gone.

Once again, his mind was acute. The problems he faced now were real, but not remotely as emotionally stultifying as standing at the bedside trying to regulate an uncontrolled heart rate. In a way, he saw himself now practicing medicine vicariously. He embraced the mental challenge without having to look a patient in the eye, or thread a spinal needle into the back, or wonder whether the penicillin he ordered would cause an anaphylactic reaction—without the worry that he would make a mistake, and a patient would die.

Now his job was to joust with practicing doctors over proposed health care services and determine whether they were covered by insurance. He had never abandoned the principle he had learned in medical school of *Primum non nocere:* First, do no harm. He had known throughout his career that *any* treatment was not necessarily a good treatment. If it was unproven by scientific studies and could cause potential harm to a patient, it was not appropriate. His job was not to tell a doctor it could not be attempted. Rather, his responsibility was to discuss whether it was demonstrated to be *the* standard of care, and, therefore, paid for by insurance.

He thought back to a recent call from an orthopedic surgeon. The physician had spent a year in Switzerland where he had learned a novel technique to repair a herniated disk. Unfortunately, it was a very new idea—no solid, scientific studies had validated it—and it was not used in the United States. Luke advised him that it was not considered the standard of care. It was unproven and therefore not a covered benefit. The surgeon was enraged.

He opined that physicians in the United States had not caught up with recent technology. He railed against the insurance company and condemned Luke as an unthinking bureaucrat, whose only concern was to deny coverage.

Luke picked up the phone.

This is Dr. Lawrence at the Southeast Cancer Institute. Are you the medical director? The caller's tone of voice was controlled anger.

Yes. My name is Dr. Luke James.

Well, my patient has metastatic breast cancer and has failed chemotherapy. She needs a bone-marrow transplant. I understand you have denied coverage because you consider the procedure experimental. His voice had begun to rise and became both condescending and accusatory.

Luke responded.

Dr. Lawrence, I am not aware of any studies in the medical literature that have shown bone marrow transplantation to be effective in metastatic breast cancer. So, yes. The procedure is considered experimental or unproven, and as such, not a covered benefit.

Dr. Lawrence interrupted.

Where do you get off telling me what is unproven? Are you an oncologist?

No, I'm not. I am trained in Pulmonary Medicine, but I am certainly familiar with the medical literature.

So where did you do your training?

Why is that relevant?

It matters because here at Southeast, we are considered experts at this. Not all medical schools are, and I need to know what kind of training you had that makes you an expert.

Luke replied, I don't claim to be an expert, but I am very familiar with the medical literature on this topic.

The caller was adamant.

I need to know where you trained.

Luke could not see the point, but conceded.

OK, if it's important to you, I trained at Harvard.

There was a pregnant pause. Luke broke the silence.

Now can we discuss this case?

The oncologist's voice softened. After several minutes of collegial discussion, he acquiesced.

Look, we've run out of ideas to treat this lady. Her prognosis, as you know, is awful. We'll have to rethink the options and call you back.

Luke hung up the phone and sat in the dusk. He let the conversation wash over him. His thoughts took him back to a cold January night during his internship. The memory of Maria Gonsalves was still fresh. He had argued, then, that doing a total body washout was her only hope for survival. It failed, and she died. The procedure had never caught on and was now a distant memory.

Ironically, he knew then that the procedure was unproven—hopeful, at best—based on experience with a few patients. In fact, the procedure itself may have hastened her death by a few days or weeks. Like the oncologist on the phone, he had been willing to try anything. He vividly recalled Jean Fortier, the gentle soul who died of leukemia. He remembered donating white blood cells in a frantic attempt to forestall the inevitable, fully aware that the procedure was unproven. It was a ray of hope.

Looking back, he could see that his emotional investment had distorted his scientific judgment. He knew that medical knowledge was built brick by brick on a foundation of hard facts. But he also discovered early that patients are sentient beings, and as a new doctor, his decisions often became clouded with emotion. When it happened, rigid medical science took a backseat.

His thoughts brought him back to the present. Oncologists who dealt with terminal cancer were, like him, trained to be medical scientists. They honed their skills with strict adherence to the scientific method. The days of alchemy and blood-letting had given way to contemporary medicine. As hard as it was, to be mindful of the principle, *First, do no harm,* sometimes meant deciding that it was better to offer no treatment at all than to offer a patient treatment that was unproven—that could make a patient worse, or even kill them.

But even long after the naiveté of internship, the cry from a dying patient, *Doc, there must be something,* fell on sympathetic ears. Desperation led people to spend their life savings on therapies hawked by charlatans. Apricot extracts, coffee enemas, unpalatable formulations of greenish liquids at remote cancer spas. Homes remortgaged, money borrowed. Bills left to be paid after they died, which they all did. All because they could not get past the idea that something must be better than nothing.

We were all trained to be objective, to stand back and not let emotion cloud our judgment. The oncologist from Southeastern was no different. He would have been taught that it was critically important to know if and when approaches to treatment were proven to be effective and appropriate.

He repeated the words to himself: *We were all taught to be objective.* It was not enough to know that some cancer specialist had treated a group of women with a particular combination of drugs, radiation, and surgery that seemed to work. Compared with what? Was the outcome better for certain combinations than others? More important, had the outcomes of patients receiving one type of therapy been compared with the outcomes of those receiving another? Ultimately, did receiving any type of therapy versus none at all make any appreciable difference in the outcome?

We were all taught that to offer a treatment that hastened the death of a patient was worse than not treating at all. Even doctors in training knew that any treatment that would hasten the death of a patient was not acceptable. So, all approaches to treatment had to undergo the rigor of scientific proof. This became a maxim that must be adhered to. It became the immutable approach that drove medical knowledge.

He drew a breath and thought about the lady with breast cancer. The diagnostic part was easy. A biopsy was taken and was reviewed under a microscope by the pathologist. Malignant cells were seen, growing faster and more disorganized than the surrounding normal tissue. The next step was to stage the cancer. Cancer cells spread first through the lymph nodes of the axilla. A surgeon harvested the lymph nodes. If cancer was seen, where else was it—in the lung or liver or bone marrow? In her case the answer was yes to all. She had Stage Four breast cancer. It was all over her body.

Then came the treatment. What to do? Should she be advised to have a total mastectomy? Should the other breast be removed to prevent spread of the malignant cells? Should radiation be considered? How about chemotherapy? What kind, how much, how long?

Luke knew that his oncology sparring partner had learned to ask these questions, then formulate a treatment plan based on proven medical studies. Mastectomy was deforming. Radiation therapy caused skin breakdown. Chemotherapy would make her sick with vomiting, diarrhea, total physical exhaustion. All these, and many more considerations had to be made. A bone marrow transplant could kill her.

Throughout his career the practicing physician had to sit across from each patient and read the fear and hope in their eyes. Science took a backseat, just as it had when he was a young intern. It became far more difficult behind the exam room door, talking to a patient he had come to know—her family, her history, her need to hang onto life at all cost. How could a doctor look at a patient and say, *There is no proof. You have a disease that will end your life. No treatment will help.*

Was strict adherence to science incompatible with empathy? Did the specter of death lead Dr. Lawrence to recommend an unproven procedure because the fear of death trumped objectivity? Had he gone too far down one track and replaced science with emotion?

Suddenly it occurred to Luke that perhaps he was no one to sit in judgment. Wasn't it he who recommended all those years ago that Maria Gonsalves have her blood replaced in a desperate effort to save her? Wasn't it he who donated white blood cells to Jean Fortier in an unproven attempt to save his life?

He knew too well the pain of telling the truth, how saying to a patient *there is no hope* takes its toll—and he knew it back at the beginning. He knew too well that doctors were never criticized for doing something, anything, proven or not. It was when they declared that it was time to do nothing that the critics came out of the woodwork.

Luke argued to himself that he had not lost empathy when he allowed Lucille Cartwright to die peacefully. To the contrary, it was a moment when he truly joined the science and the art of medicine. And his reward was a lawsuit that nearly destroyed him. The voice of the plaintiff's attorney continued to ring in his ears. *You let her die.* Only now was he beginning to heal from the pain of being condemned for providing comfort when no treatment would help.

He stared at the phone and thought about his recent conversation with Dr. Lawrence. He gazed out at the darkening sky from his comfortable office, high above the city and far from the world he'd once inhabited. He knew he needed to talk to doctors about science and proof. That was his job. *It's only verbal jousting.*

It took a lot of energy to try to get doctors to remember those principles they all had learned. He was acutely aware of the most basic drive of all living beings: to stay alive. And for humans, the instinct was complicated by rational thought.

He pledged never to forget the pain and isola-tion of sitting across from a tearful patient, clinging tenaciously to this basic need. Practitioners like Dr. Lawrence, and like Luke himself, were torn constantly between the need to be loyal to science without abandoning empathy. The ongoing challenge would be for every doctor to find the nexus between art and science. This was the practice of medicine.

The long day was over. It was time to head home. Luke put on his coat and turned out the light.

Dear Reader

A Doctor a Day is a novel about one practicing physician's experience with the constant, unrelenting care of dying patients, and the physical, emotional and psychological consequences. The pressure becomes unbearable when he is sued for malpractice, leading him to consider suicide as the only escape. Though the story is fictional, it reflects real-life issues faced by practicing physicians.

Why did I write this novel? My major goal was to provide insight for the lay public into the mind of a physician by following Luke, a physician, through the tenth year of his medical practice. It serves to unmask the psychological burden experienced by Luke, as an example—albeit extreme—of what physicians experience during their careers.

Sadly, the suicide rate among doctors is fifty percent greater than the general population. The need for doctors to maintain an air of infallibility to show strength to their patients is certainly contributory.

The mental health support system for doctors is severely lacking. All of these issues lead to the important question, "Who heals the healer?"

I hope that you find the story interesting and thought-provoking.

Thank you for reading *A Doctor a Day*,

—Bernard Mansheim

Suggested Book Club Questions

1. The major theme of the novel is the question *"Who heals the healer."* Did the author effectively raise this issue? What are other ways to address this issue?

2. One obvious sub-theme worthy of discussion is the problem of physician suicide, which occurs at a rate 1. 5 that of the general population. Were you aware of this fact before reading this book? If so, how — through personal experience? Or reading about it in journals? Or by watching information programs such as *TEDMED Talks*?

3. Another sub-theme is the notion that medical practice is the nexus between the art and science of medicine. Did the author make this clear and what are some examples in the text?

4. Medical malpractice is another sub-theme. What did you learn about its potential psychological impact on doctors?

5. The author wrote about the unequal distribution of health care access among various socio-economic groups. What are your opinions about society's obligation to provide health care for everyone?

6. There were multiple sub-themes found in the novel. Were they effectively woven into the story?

7. Luke felt trapped with no way out. Why do you suppose he felt unable to get help or to reach out for help?

8. Did you empathize with Luke? Or were you sympathetic?

9. The author chose to eliminate quotes in the dialogue. Why do you think he did so? Was it effective?

10. Discuss how the mood of the story is set by the use of third-person limited narration (i.e., thoughts and feelings are provided by the protagonist, Luke). Was it effective in conveying emotion? Mood? Urgency? Despondency?

11. Did the various patient anecdotes help to explain the psychological pressure experienced by Luke? Which ones stood out to you?

12. Did the novel give you any new insight into the practice of medicine and contemporary healthcare?

13. What do you think of Luke's decision to remove himself from direct contact from patients by working with healthcare insurance providers after his confrontation with suicide and with the malpractice lawsuit?

14. Can you relate Luke's experience to anyone who you know—physician or not?

15. Do you agree with Luke's decision to provide comfort when no treatment would help? Have you had to make this decision for a loved one?

Acknowledgements

I would like to express my appreciation for the manuscript review by Chanticleer Reviews. They provided the incentive to complete *A Doctor a Day*, my first novel.

The excellent contributions of my editors, especially S.J.S. Stanton, cannot be overstated. They kept the story on a succinct path to completion, and offered valuable advice based on long experience.

I am indebted to Kathryn Brown and her associates at Sillan Pace Brown for publishing my novel.

Finally, I want to express my deepest gratitude to my wife, as she quietly supported my literary effort.

Bernard Mansheim, M.D.

Please visit my website at
www.BernardMansheim.com
for more information about this topic and for
updates regarding my next works in the
Everydoctor Series.

Made in the USA
Columbia, SC
17 December 2017